PUPPY LOVE

PUPPY
LOVE

Jeanne Betancourt

AN AVON CAMELOT BOOK

PUPPY LOVE is an original publication of Avon Books. This work
has never before appeared in book form.

AVON BOOKS
A division of
The Hearst Corporation
1790 Broadway
New York, New York 10019

Copyright © 1986 by Jeanne Betancourt
Published by arrangement with the author
Library of Congress Catalog Card Number: 85-21468
ISBN: 0-380-89958-2
RL: 4.2

Library of Congress Cataloging in Publication Data

Betancourt, Jeanne.
  Puppy love

  Summary: A child of divorced parents, eighth-grader
Aviva has to deal with her two families, a new baby
brother, grief over her dog's death, a crush on an
unattainable boy, and a troubled schoolmate who turns
out to be a really good friend and strong support.
  [1. Remarriage--Fiction.   2. Friendship--Fiction]
I. Title.
PZ7.B46626Pu 1986   [Fic]   85-21468

First Camelot Printing, May 1986

CAMELOT TRADEMARK REG. U.S. PAT. OFF. AND IN
OTHER COUNTRIES, MARCA REGISTRADA, HECHO EN
U.S.A.

Printed in the U. S. A.

OPM 10 9 8 7 6 5 4 3 2

In memory of my father, Henry Granger,
Aviva's first fan.

CHAPTER ONE

FOR EIGHTH GRADE WE GOT THE TEACHER WE knew we'd be getting. Mrs. Petronella Peterson. Anyone who'd graduated from St. Agnes in the last thirty-five years had Mrs. Petronella Peterson for eighth grade.

When we came into Room 306 the seats were already labeled with our names. I knew enough to go right to the back of the room. There I was—last seat, last row—"Miss Aviva Granger." And right next to me in the second-to-last row, last seat—"Mr. Josh Greene." I looked around as the starting bell rang. "Mr. Josh Greene" wasn't there.

"Ladies and gentlemen," Mrs. Peterson began with a rap of her wooden pointer on the blackboard. We all sat at attention. Two more quick taps on the board. "The school year has officially begun."

A low moan rolled through the room.

"No, no," Mrs. Peterson warned with a shake of her head and a shake of her stick. "Let us begin again. There is nothing to moan about. You are among the luckiest young men and women in the world. You live in a splendid city in a wonderful country. You go to an excellent school. It is your responsibility to learn. It is my responsibility to teach you. I will teach. You will learn. And no one will moan. We have a great deal of work to do together, class. Let us begin."

She pulled herself up to make her five feet a bit taller, tugged on the jacket of her navy-blue suit so there weren't any wrinkles, gave us a serious look and repeated, "Ladies and gentlemen. The school year has begun." She tapped on the board again—three loud taps.

No one moaned. Not out loud anyway.

At that moment Josh Greene opened the door and walked in. Ronnie Cioffi chuckled. But Mrs. Peterson let it go. All of her attention was focused on Josh, who stood eleven

1

inches above her. "Good morning, Mr. Greene," she said without any scolding in her voice. She was friendly and not annoyed the way I thought she would be. After all, he had a reputation for being the toughest kid in school, she had a reputation for being the strictest teacher, and he was late on the first day of school. The other surprise was that Josh wasn't fresh or anything. He just looked around and said, "Sorry I'm late."

They met halfway across the room. She handed him a file card and said, "Please copy this form on the board while I pass out the students' copies." While Mrs. P.P. counted out file cards for the first person in each row to pass back, Josh went to the board and carefully printed "Name" and "Address" and other stuff like that, and drew neat lines for the spaces.

I studied Josh from the back. I hadn't seen him since the end of the school year. I spent the summer at sleepaway camp and he . . . well, I didn't know what he'd been doing. Probably getting taller and walking dogs, which is what he does for a living. He used to walk my dog Mop before he died. Anyway, what you couldn't help noticing about Josh on the first day of school was that he had on this orange rayon shirt that said "Windsor Monuments" in purple embroidered letters. Under the words there was an outline of a tombstone. It was really hard not to laugh.

I watched Cioffi three rows over and two rows down. He was doubled over in pain from trying to squelch a big hoot. But Josh kept a straight face when he turned around from drawing the model card on the board and took seven long strides down the aisle to his place.

"Now, ladies and gentlemen," Mrs. P.P. said as she picked up a piece of chalk. "Take out your pens and we will fill in these cards together."

Josh slipped into his seat and stuck a leg out in each aisle.

2

"Gimme a pen," were the first words Josh Greene said to me in the eighth grade.

Josh thinks of me as his personal stationery supplier, but this year I was prepared. I handed him a pen I'd bought at a toy store over the summer. It had a little Smurf on the top of it. You know, the kind of pen you'd give a first–grade girl. He looked at it, looked at me, and whispered, "Thanks." Then he broke the doll–part off and put it back on my desk.

Mrs. P.P. began: "The principal has asked that the first thing we do this school year is make out new emergency cards. These cards are to be used if we need to reach your parents in an emergency. A model of the card," she pointed to the board, "has been carefully duplicated for you by Mr. Greene. I will guide you as you fill out your cards. Pens positioned. Begin."

As Mrs. P.P. gave directions I started to fill in the card. "NAME: Granger, Aviva." That was easy. But what about address? I live half with my dad and half with my mom. One week with one, and then one week with the other. That's two addresses right there. But it's even more complicated. In a week my dad and I were moving in with his girlfriend, Miriam the Moron. So that's three addresses. I decided to use two addresses—Mom's and Miriam's—and write real small. Only problem was I didn't know the house number for Miriam's, which is understandable since we don't live there yet. So I put Miriam's street without the number.

Parents' names and office numbers were also a problem. My mother married her boyfriend George and now her name is Jan O'Connell. I hate that. Wouldn't the school get confused now that she and I have different last names? And was I supposed to put in George's office number, too? And what about Miriam's work number since I'd be living with her? What if there were an emergency and they couldn't reach my mom or dad? I left Miriam's out because I didn't know it anyway. And squeezed George's in.

The next line was SIBLINGS. That was easy. I made a big fat "O." My mom and George were having a baby, but they didn't have it yet and it really wasn't going to be my whole brother because George wasn't my father.

Even without any siblings my card was pretty crowded.

I looked over to see how Josh was doing. He'd taken back the Smurf doll from my desk and was drawing little tattoos all over it with the pen. His card was on the upper left-hand corner of the desk, where Mrs. P.P. had told us to put them. I read it.

NAME: Greene, Josh

ADDRESS: St. Joseph's Home for Boys
North Ave. Burlington, Vermont

MOTHER'S NAME AND WORK NUMBER: None
                                None
FATHER'S NAME AND WORK NUMBER: None
                                None
IN CASE OF EMERGENCY CONTACT: My job at
Angelo's Animal Care (785-9842) - or -
Father Tierney at St. Joe's

That Josh was at St. Joseph's orphanage wasn't news to me. His grandmother had died just before the school year was over. We all went to the funeral. It was awful. Maybe that's why Mrs. P.P. didn't give him a hard time for being late. His mother died when he was little and his dad just

4

disappeared. I don't know which happened first, the mother dying or the dad disappearing.

Josh Greene didn't have any "parents" and I had too many. Wouldn't it be wonderful, I thought, if I could give Miriam and George to Josh. George and Josh knew one another from all the times Josh was at my house to walk Mop when I was at my dad's. George thinks Josh is this terrific kid. They even do things together, like fishing and stuff. So it was a perfect plan. George and Miriam would be Josh's parents and I would have my parents back together in our old house. We'd be a family. They'd be a family. They could even have the new baby. If my mother missed it, we could make it a joint-custody baby. Baby would live half the time with Mom and Dad and me and the other half of the time with George, Miriam, and Josh.

"Miss Granger?"

I didn't even hear Mrs. P.P. coming up the aisle. I took my elbow off the card and handed it to her. She looked it over. "Your mother was a fine student. I understand that you take after her. This will be a good school year for you."

Josh was making an expression like a Smurf doll at me from behind Mrs. P.P. I practically bit my tongue off trying not to laugh. As she turned to him his face transformed from silly Smurf to serious student. She picked up his card. "Your father, Thomas, was in my class," she said in a low voice. But she didn't say anything embarrassing like, "Why didn't you put his name on the card?" Or, "Where is he living now?"

As she added the card to the pile she said, "You're a very bright young man, Mr. Greene. I expect you to use your God-given gifts. It's my job to see you do."

"Yes, ma'am," Josh answered.

"I'm happy to see that you're working for Angelo. But you mustn't let your after-school job interfere with your schoolwork. Do you understand?"

5

"Yes, ma'am," Josh said.

She turned with a sigh and headed to the front of the room. I guess she figured she had her work cut out for her with our class. She'd have known for sure that she did if she'd seen Josh and me making Smurf faces at one another behind her back.

After school, Sue, Louise, and I headed toward Sammy's, the pizza place, where a lot of the kids from our school and the high school hang out. "Summer's over," Sue said. "I just can't believe it. Can you believe it, Aviva? I mean, can you *really* believe that we're the eighth graders now?"

"I'm not so sure I like being the oldest in the school," Louise said as she shifted her heavy bookbag from one shoulder to the other. "It's like there aren't any guys left. I mean there's nobody to *like* in our class."

"Well, we have Josh to entertain us," Sue said. "At least he's funny."

"Yeah, he's funny," I said. "If you don't have to sit next to him."

We looked into Sammy's before we went in. Lots of kids were there—mostly from the high school—including a whole group from last year's eighth grade. There were kids from our school, too, like some sixth-grade boys who were fooling around and being obnoxious. Sue and Louise were discussing where we should sit when we went in so we wouldn't be standing in the middle looking for a booth or anything stupid like that.

I studied our reflections in the window to see if we looked different from last year. Sue was one whole inch taller, but still the shortest kid in the class. She'd cut her dark curly hair real short and wore neat, aqua shell-shaped earrings. Louise looked the same. She'd looked like she was in eighth grade since fifth grade! And I looked pretty much the same. But I thought my jacket was neat looking—an old, red satin basketball player's jacket. It was my mother's from before she was pregnant and too big for all her clothes.

I'd started to wear makeup over the summer, but didn't wear any on the first day of school because I knew Josh Greene would say something embarrassing in front of everyone like, "Hey, you got dirt on your eye," or "Is your lip bleeding?" Maybe I could wear makeup to school if I did it gradually. A little bit more each day, so it wouldn't be so noticeable. Louise had on loads of makeup.

"How long can you stay?" Sue asked me as we went through the swinging door into Sammy's.

"Until four," I answered. "I promised to help with supper. That was before I knew we were going to have ten thousand hours of homework on the first night."

I smiled at Sue as we acted like we were talking about the most important thing in the world, so everyone at Sammy's would know that we were lively, interesting people.

"Louise. Over here," Rita called from a booth in the back. She was sitting with a couple of guys and a girl from last year's eighth grade. One of the guys was *Bob Hanley*. My heart pounded as the three of us walked over to the booth. Maybe I'd sit next to him.

"I guess I could stay a little later," I whispered to Sue as we reached the booth.

"Gee, there's only room for one of you," Rita said looking straight at Louise and tugging on her so she'd sit down before Sue or I did.

Bob Hanley moved over to make room for Louise. He looked up at us and asked, "How's it going over at St. Aggie's?"

"Good," I said.

"Real good," Sue added.

" 'Scuse me," the waitress said as she bumped past Sue and me to put a pizza deluxe down in the middle of their

7

table. "Think you could find a seat, girls? You're blocking traffic here."

"Bye," we said. They said good-bye back, but without looking up or anything. They were already dividing up the pizza.

Sue and I went to the counter and ordered two slices to go and got out of there.

I was home by three-thirty.

"Myrtle, I'm home!" I called out as soon as I came into the kitchen. I dropped my bookbag on the table and went into my bedroom to see how she was doing. She was doing what she usually does. Nothing. Just lying there in her box. Sometimes she'll waddle from the roaster-pan-pond part to the dry part, but only when no one's looking. Pet turtles can be pretty boring.

I went back to the living room and turned on the TV to keep me company and called my mom at work to let her know I was home. It took her a while to get to the phone. I was ready to tell her about Mrs. Peterson and all the homework, but Mom was too full of her own news to listen.

"Oh, Aviva," she said excitedly. "They're giving me the most wonderful baby shower! This baby is going to have the cutest things. I just opened a little T-shirt with a rainbow on it when they told me you were on the phone. Isn't that amazing? Your symbol and you were calling me at that very instant."

"Yeah," I said, "but rainbows aren't my symbol anymore, Mom. I'm in the eighth grade and . . ."

She interrupted me. "I've got to go back, honey. Everyone's waiting for me to finish opening the gifts. You'll love all these cute things."

"Mom," I caught her before she hung up. "What's for supper? This morning you said I should cook it."

"Never mind. You probably have a lot of homework. Be-

8

sides, George said he'd make us chicken with cashews to celebrate my last day at the office and everything. I'll be home in another hour or so. Gotta go. Love you."

She hung up.

I watched a soap opera and a "Little House on the Prairie" rerun while I did the easiest homework. James was going into a burning barn to get the animals out, and I was in the middle of a multiplication–of–fractions problem, when George came home.

The back door opened and then banged closed. I heard the bags of groceries plop on the counter. "Aviva," he called. "I'm home."

I yelled back a hi.

He stood in the doorway between the kitchen and living room. "Did your mother tell you about the baby shower?" he asked.

"Uh-huh."

"Sounds like she got a lot of loot. How about you? How was school?"

This is what George always does if he gets home from work before Mom: talk to me and start supper. Sometimes I say I have a lot of homework to do, turn off the TV, and go to my room. Other times I answer his questions and help him cook. That night I didn't do either because just then Mom got home and I had to help her carry in the baby presents. Then I had to look at everything.

She sat in my dad's old easy chair and showed us all the presents, one by one. The clothes were so little and her belly was so big and she was *so* excited. George was, too.

"Here it is, sweetie," she said as she opened a small, flat, white box and separated the yellow tissue paper. "Ta-ta!" She held up this itsy-bitsy undershirt with a rainbow painted across it. A real silly rainbow with a pot of gold at the end of it.

"What do you think?"

9

I smiled at her. "That's nice, Mom," I said. "Real cute."

"And he's kicking. Right now. Feel."

She took my hand and put it on her belly. The baby gave my hand a big kick. My mom was always doing this. Trying to get me involved with the baby she and George were going to have.

CHAPTER TWO

DaD 14 M	DaD 15 T	DaD 16 W	DaD 17 T	DaD 18 F	DaD 19 S	DaD 20 S

MONDAYS ARE MY MOVING DAYS—THE DAY I GO back to my dad's when I'm at mom's or when I go back to my mom's when I'm at my dad's. This is how it works: Monday, before I go to school, I leave all the stuff I want for the next week packed and at the front door. After school I go to the other house, open the door and there's my suitcase and Myrtle in her box at the front door. This is how it gets from house to house: My dad does it.

Except this week at Dad's we were *really* moving—from our apartment into Miriam's condominium.

"Did you measure all your furniture?" Dad yelled out to me as he came down the hall toward my room.

I was sitting at my desk trying to come up with some ideas for a "creative essay" for Mrs. P.P. We were supposed to make an inanimate thing animate. Like pretending a hammer or a chair could think. I thought maybe I'd do a pencil, but I was having a lot of trouble coming up with any ideas of what a pencil would think or do if it were alive. What I wished was that it could write my creative essay for me.

As Dad came in my room I turned my paper over so he wouldn't see the only thing I'd written on the paper:

Now that was creative! Bob would never, not in ten million years, end up in a heart with me.

Dad looked over my shoulder at the blank page. "You haven't measured one piece of furniture," he said. "Look, I did all mine." Dad proudly held up a yellow pad filled with the measurements for our furniture.

"I have homework to do," I explained.

"Miriam's expecting us for supper." He looked at his watch. "Right now. Meatloaf. You'll love it. You can do your homework after dinner." He looked around my crowded little room. "But I promised her we'd have our measurements. Here, I'll help you." He pulled out the end of the measuring tape and laid it across my bureau. "Write this down. 'Bureau 2'5" width.' "

I stuffed the Aviva and Bob page in my bookbag. "Dad," I said as I stood up. "My room at Miriam's is about twice the size of this one. My furniture will fit. Trust me. Let's just get going."

He put his arm around my shoulder. "You're right," he

said. "And you can fix it up just the way you want." As we walked out of the room and down the hall he added, "I mean, as long as it's okay with Miriam."

This is what our apartment is like: small and homey. And ours.

This is what Miriam's condominium is like: big and cluttered. And hers.

Monday night we had a pretty good meatloaf at Miriam's and talked about where our furniture would go. All the time Dad and Miriam were making lovey-dovey eyes at one another.

Tuesday night Dad and I packed our stuff in boxes.

Wednesday night Dad and I packed our stuff in boxes.

Thursday night Dad packed our stuff in boxes and I finally wrote my creative essay. I wrote about my sheepdog, Mop, who was killed by a car. In the essay I had him come back to life and be with me again. I didn't know if it was what Mrs. P.P. meant by inanimate becoming animate, but I didn't care. I wrote it anyway. I cried as I remembered my wonderful dog and wrote him back to life. But I felt good, too, because writing about Mop made it seem like he was in the room with me, at least for a little while. I could smell his great doggy smell, feel his fluffy coat, and mostly, see the love in his eyes.

"Aviva." My dad was knocking on my bedroom door.

I wiped the tears off my face and called, "What?"

He walked in as I turned around. "Look what I found under the couch," he said. He held out a chewed-up red sneaker that was mine when I was about four years old and had been Mop's favorite chew thing. Dad's eyes were wet with tears and the tears came back to my eyes. I took the shoe from him. I knew I'd keep it forever. No matter how many times we moved.

"How's your essay coming along?" he asked. "It's getting pretty lonely out there."

"I finished," I told him as I handed him the essay. He read it.

"You know, pumpkin," Dad said when he finished, "there's no rule against dogs in Miriam's building. After we've settled in there you could have another dog. One you can keep at both places." He patted me on the head. "I mean, if it's all right with Miriam."

"I could never have another dog," I told him. "No dog could replace Mop." I glanced at Myrtle lying in the same spot she'd been in for ten hours. "Besides, I have Myrtle."

"I understand," Dad said. "Just thought I'd mention it."

Saturday morning Dad's friend Louie helped us load all our stuff into this rented truck. Miriam didn't help because she works in her store Saturdays. She used to teach home economics in my dad's college, but now she has her own store, a boutique called Miriam's Magic.

My job on moving day was to carry the not-so-heavy boxes to the truck and to sweep each room after we'd moved all the stuff out. I was feeling sad about leaving even though we'd only lived there two years. I mean it was our first place after the divorce and all. I wished, after I swept my room, that Louie and Dad would just move the stuff right back in and we could go back to normal. I figured Dad could stay at Miriam's the weeks I was at Mom's. He'd have two homes like me. Miriam and I would have joint custody of Dad!

I put my broom down and went to the elevator to wait for Dad to come back. I'd decided to tell him this idea and that I didn't want to move. My palms were all sweaty with nervousness as I listened to the elevator coming up the shaft.

As it stopped at our floor I heard Dad say to Louie, "I really love that girl, Lou. I'd do anything for her." My heart thump, thumped. If he loved me so much that he'd tell his friend maybe I could keep us from moving into Miriam's.

14

The elevator doors slid open.

"Dad," I said with a big smile. "Can I talk to you?" I glanced at Louie. "Private."

"I'll start the kitchen," Louie said as he pushed the empty hand truck off the elevator. "Boy, Aviva," he said as he clanked it down the hall. "You got your hands full with your dad. He's a fool in love. This Miriam must be something else."

"So," Dad said when Louie was out of earshot. "What is it?"

I swallowed hard. "Nothing. I mean, I just wanted to tell you I was finished sweeping my room . . . and . . ." I did some fast thinking. ". . . And that you said you'd call Miriam at twelve." I pointed to his watch. "It's twelve-thirty."

By six o'clock all our stuff was in Miriam's apartment and I didn't care where I lived, just as long as I didn't have to lift one more box.

I was lying in what space was left on the floor of the living room and Dad was sprawled out on our couch which was parked right in front of Miriam's couch.

"I may die here," Dad said. "Just like this. Starved, overworked. My muscles hugging my bones in pain."

"Oh . . ." I moaned. I didn't have enough energy left to put my misery into words.

We didn't even budge when we heard Miriam open the front door. Neither of us could get up.

"Welcome," she yelled from the hall. Then she bounced into the room, all pretty and clean, in a red Miriam's Magic outfit. In one hand she had a bunch of daisies, in the other a bag of Chinese food.

We groaned hellos, but didn't budge. In fact we didn't even wait for her to put the food on her pretty plates. We didn't even let her take it out of the bags. "Gimmie a fork,"

Dad called from the couch where he was eating chicken and broccoli. "It's faster than chopsticks."

As I ate I watched Miriam put on her striped chef's apron, arrange the daisies in a vase, put some food on one of her rose-edged plates, and start to daintily manipulate the chopsticks. After she took a few bites she said, "Why don't you two just go to bed when you've finished eating and we'll deal with all of this in the morning." She looked around at our piles of boxes and furniture and sighed. Then she pushed her chair back. "All we have to do is set up Aviva's bed."

"I'll help," I said as I took a last bite of fried rice and closed the bag. I stood up. Dad didn't say a word.

Miriam and I went around to the other side of the couch and looked at him. He hadn't heard a word she said. He was fast asleep, holding an unopened fortune cookie in one hand and a fork in the other.

"We can do it," I told Miriam. "Let him sleep."

"You know how?" Miriam asked. "I mean how to put a bed together."

"Sure," I said. "It's easy."

I was surprised that they didn't teach Miriam how to put a bed together in home economics school.

When we'd finished I sat on it and it didn't fall apart, which is how you test if you did it right.

"We did it," Miriam said. "Great!" She sat on the bed next to me. "You know, Aviva," she said, "I'm glad you moved in. I always wanted a younger sister. We can have fun together."

"Right," I said. "It's a nice apartment." I looked Miriam straight in the eye when I added, "And Dad said I could have a dog here."

Her eyes sort of glazed over and she bit her lower lip. That's when I knew my having a dog would be a true test of her love for my dad.

CHAPTER THREE

SEPTEMBER

MoM	MoM	MoM	MoM	MoM	MoM	MoM
21 M	22 T	23 W	24 T	25 F	26 S	27 S

"WHAT'D YOU DO YOUR ESSAY ON?" EVERYONE was asking everyone else at lunch on Monday.

"A telephone," Louise said as she pulled apart her grilled cheese sandwich to put in some ketchup. "I have my telephone talk back to me. It knows everything I know because it's in on all my conversations. We talk for hours—me and my telephone. For the essay I make it a Pooh Bear phone so you can really picture it talking."

"That's neat," Sue said. "I wish I'd thought of it."

"So what'd you use?" Rita asked her.

"Boring," Sue said as she took a last sip of her milk and shook her curly head of hair. "I don't like it at all. Just this old picture of my grandmother that's in my room of when she was my age. She talks to me from the picture and tells me all about when she was a kid, only she is a kid. Know what I mean?"

"That's a good idea," Rita said without a trace of enthusiasm.

I didn't want to tell them that I wrote about Mop. It was too personal and besides I didn't think it was what the teacher meant for us to do. I'd probably get a failing grade.

"I hope she has us read them out loud," Rita said.

"And I hope," Louise added, "that she doesn't have us tell what it is, make everybody guess. You know, you'd just say 'blank' or 'teakettle' or something whenever you got to the thing." She took a bite of her sandwich. "What'd you use, Aviva?"

I was already praying that Mrs. P.P. wouldn't have us

17

read our essays out loud. "I'm not saying," I told my friends. "In case she does what you said, Louise. I don't want anyone to know."

"Oh," moaned Sue. "I wish I hadn't told."

Tuesday, after lunch, Mrs. P.P. stood in front of the class with our essays piled in her hands. "Well, class," she said. "I've graded your first essays and I must say this class gets an 'A' for imagination."

We all smiled at one another. Quietly. Maybe eighth grade wouldn't be so terrible after all.

"And," she added as she moved closer, "this class gets a 'D' for good English. I have never seen so many careless errors in a set of papers in my thirty-five years of teaching." She looked us over. "We certainly have our work cut out for us this year."

The smiles disappeared.

While we did a grammar exercise in our English workbook, identifying the parts of speech, Mrs. P.P. passed back our essays. At least we didn't have to read them out loud.

When she got to the back of the room she put a paper on my desk and a paper on Josh's. I took a quick look. I had "A-" for content and a "B" for mechanics—like spelling and grammar.

"I find it curious," she said, looking from me to Josh and back again, "that you both chose the same subject. Since you handled it so differently I'm not splitting the grade. In the future, however, I expect you to come up with your own ideas for creative writing. Do you understand?"

Josh and I looked at one another and shrugged shoulders. What was she talking about? As soon as her back was turned we exchanged essays.

I couldn't believe it. Josh had written about Mop, too. Only he had a better opening. In my essay I come in the door and Mop is just there, greeting me with happy yelps and kisses like he always did. In Josh's essay, he's holding Mop's old leash and thinking about him. All of a sudden, Mop appears at the end of his leash. I didn't even know Josh had the leash. I never thought of where Mop's leash went the day that Josh was walking him and he got hit by a car. Maybe, I thought, if I had Mop's leash I would have come up with an opening like that.

"Mine's better," Josh said when we exchanged papers back. And he was right.

"No it isn't," I said.

"You ever been to Angelo's?" Josh asked when we were packing up our books to go home on Wednesday.

"Uh-uh," I answered. "We take—took—Mop to Jack Martin in South Burlington."

"Wanna see it?" Josh asked.

"I dunno," I answered.

"Good," Josh said. "Meet me there in twenty minutes. Corner of Foster and Maple."

Before I could say, You have some nerve, or You can't tell me what to do, or I have other plans—or before anyone could notice him talking to me—Josh Greene had taken seven strides down the aisle, said "Good Afternoon" to Mrs. Peterson, and was out the door.

Actually I did have other plans—to go for pizza with Sue and Rita. But the truth was I was getting sick of spending two dollars a day to have the high school kids ignore me—especially Bob Hanley, who everyone knew was trying to get Joanne Richards to go out with him. This is what Joanne Richards looks like: Brooke Shields.

Angelo's was in a regular house. One of those offices where the people who run it live on the second floor. I went up the front steps. The door was open so I walked in.

Right away I was in a waiting room. There were faded

photographs of different kinds of dogs and cats all over the walls. A lady was there with this dog that looked as old as she did—very old. And a kid sat in the corner with a big fluffy cat on his lap. The cat didn't look sick at all and was keeping a suspicious eye on the old dog. I went to a cut-out in the wall and peeked through. A young woman was sitting at the desk in an office area, typing up some forms or something.

I gave a little cough. She looked up. "Do you have an appointment?" she asked.

"I'm here to see Josh Greene," I said, feeling real sorry I'd come at all.

She smiled at me. A row of silvery braces sparkled in the fluorescent light. "You must be Aviva," she said.

"Right," I said.

"Josh," she yelled toward the back. "She's here."

What was Josh doing telling everyone I was coming when I didn't even tell him I would?

"Send her back," another voice yelled.

"I'm Marion," the shiny-toothed woman explained as she opened the door and led me down a long corridor. "Angelo's assistant . . . and wife. Josh told us all about you." She turned to me. "I'm sorry about your dog." I'd never met the lady and she knew all about Mop!

"They're almost finished with Delilah," she said pointing to an open door at the end of the hall. "You can go in."

"Well, there she is," a man in a white coat said as I walked into the room. He looked up from putting a strip of bandage over the stitched-up belly of this *huge* Great Dane stretched out on an aluminum table. Josh was holding out strips of bandages that the man was taking from him one by one.

"This is Angelo," Josh explained.

The smells were like a real hospital. I hated it.

"Hi," I said.

As Angelo finished up he told me all about this operation the Great Dane had and how she'd get better. It was pretty sickening and I was wishing I'd gone for pizza instead of coming to Angelo's.

When they'd lifted Delilah into this enormous cage to sleep off the anesthesia, Angelo peeled off his rubber gloves and shook my hand. "Pleased to meet you. Josh has told us all about you."

"Nice to meet you," I said.

"Why don't you take Aviva out back," Angelo said with a wink to Josh.

What is going on? I wondered as I followed Josh.

"This is out back," Josh said as we stepped out on the back porch.

"So this is where you work," I said, trying to be polite. Maybe, I thought, now that he lives in an orphanage, this is like his home and he's real proud of it and stuff. "It's nice here," I added.

He pointed to five crates lined up along the porch. "These are the animals waiting for their owners," he said. He led me by the row of crates, like we were at a zoo or something, and told me about each animal.

"This is Jason," he said, pointing to a sleeping poodle with a big bandage on its belly. "He had an ulcer, but he'll get better. He's old. It happens when they're old."

"This is Isabelle." A Siamese cat looked up at us without moving. "She was just spayed so she won't have kittens. She's going home today."

The third crate had a German shepherd with a broken leg. The fourth, another cat that had been fixed.

"This," Josh said as he hunched down in front of the last crate, "is No-Name."

I squatted next to him. "No name?" I asked as I looked in at a fluffy ball of fur that yapped and jumped and licked Josh's fingers. "What's wrong with him?"

Josh lifted the pup out of the crate and handed him to me.

"Nothing," Josh said. No-Name was licking my fingers. I let him. "Nothing's wrong with him. He's all checked out, had shots and everything. We figure he's about three months old."

"Figure," I said. "Didn't his owner tell you how old he is?"

"He doesn't have an owner," Josh said. "Angelo found him on the porch yesterday morning in a cardboard box with this note stuck on top."

Josh reached in his pocket and handed me a piece of paper. I had trouble reading it because No-Name was just as curious about it as I was. He sniffed and nibbled at the note.

> I can't take care of this puppy. Please find him a good home.
> Brokenhearted

I read it twice. "How awful," I told Josh. "I wonder why Brokenhearted couldn't take care of him."

"Maybe they didn't have enough money for the food,"

Josh said as he reached over and rubbed his hand through No-Name's golden brown fur.

"Or a mother or father or husband or someone wouldn't let her keep him."

"Or wouldn't let *him* keep him," Josh said. "The owner could have been a guy."

"Right," I agreed.

No-Name licked my cheek just like Mop used to, only Mop's tongue was bigger.

"What are you going to do with him?" I asked.

"Give him to you," Josh said casually as he stood up.

"Oh, no you're not," I said as No-Name sniffed my neck. "No dog can take Mop's place."

Josh looked down at us and grinned. "Who said anything about taking Mop's place? Of course he can't. Just think of him as another kind of pet. Pretend he's a cat or a turtle. You don't think of Myrtle taking Mop's place, do you?"

"You must be kidding."

"That settles it then. No-Name is yours."

I held that pup's jaw in my hand and looked him straight in the eyes. Two shining, energetic, brown eyes—not the loving, wise look of my blue-eyed Mop. Josh was right. No way would No-Name replace Mop. He was another dog, a different dog. And it looked like he was mine.

"My mom will love having another dog," I told Josh as we headed toward my house. "Let's surprise her."

While we were walking, No-Name had fallen asleep cradled in my arms. Josh carried our bookbags and a shopping bag Angelo had given me with food and vitamins, and a pamphlet called "You and Your Puppy."

23

"How are you going to surprise her?" Josh asked as we reached my house.

"We'll open the kitchen door and let him in, but we'll wait outside. He'll find Mom and she'll get all excited and wonder whose dog it is and then we'll come in and tell her. How's that?"

"That's good," Josh agreed. "Very good."

I tickled No-Name under his chin and whispered in his ear. "We're home," I told him. "Wake up. You're going to meet my mom."

"You're not afraid he'll scare her or something, I mean because she's having a baby?" Josh whispered as he held the door open and I put the pup on the tile floor.

"She'll love it," I assured Josh.

We stood at the screen door and watched No-Name explore the kitchen. He whimpered a little and came back to the door looking for us. Maybe Mom's taking a nap or reading a book in the living room, I thought.

"Let's try the front door," I suggested.

I unlocked the front door I expected my mom to call out, "Aviva, is that you?" There wasn't a sound.

We put No-Name on the hallway carpet. This time he wasn't so shy and went right into the living room. We waited a few minutes, but still no sign of my mom.

"I wonder where she is?" I asked Josh as I went into the house. "She said she'd be here when I got home from school."

"We better be quiet," Josh said as he followed me into the empty hall.

We looked in the living room. No Mom.

We looked in the bedroom. No Mom.

We looked in the kitchen. There was a note on the kitchen table.

24

> Honey,
>   I started labor. George is
> taking me to the hospital.
> It looks like your baby brother
> will be arriving two weeks early.
> George will call you.
> Hamburger meat in frig.
>   Love,
>   M♡M

"Oh, boy," Josh said. "Your mom's having the baby. You'll have a brother."

"I don't want a brother," I told Josh. "Besides, he won't *really* be my brother anyway." I looked around. "Hey, where's No-Name?"

We looked around the kitchen. No No-Name.

We looked in the living room. No No-Name.

We looked in my mother's bedroom. There was No-Name going to the bathroom in the middle of my mother's rug.

"How do we get him to do it outside?" I asked Josh as I tried to clean the rug.

"I don't know," Josh said.

"You work for a veterinarian," I said. "You're supposed to know things like that."

"You had a dog," Josh said. "You're supposed to know things like that."

"Mop always knew what to do," I answered as I looked

25

at the big, brown stain in the middle of my mother's pink-flowered rug. "And where to do it," I added.

"That's impossible," Josh said as he sat there watching me and playing with No-Name. "How old were you when you got Mop?"

"Four," I answered.

"See," Josh said. "You just don't remember. Your mom and dad must have trained him."

"I wonder how long Mom will have to stay in the hospital?" I said. "I'm going to need her help."

The phone rang.

I ran to answer it. Josh and No-Name followed.

It was George.

"Well, Aviva," he said. "The baby's not here yet, but things are going along nicely, very nicely."

"That's nice," I answered.

"Looks like it'll be a few more hours. I'll call you the minute he's born. Okay?"

"Okay."

"Your mom sends her love."

"Me, too," I said. "I mean I send her my love."

"I'll tell her," he said. "Are you all right there alone?"

"Josh is here," I told him.

"Josh? Terrific. Maybe he'll eat supper with you. That would be nice."

"Okay," I said. "Bye."

"Want to stay for supper?" I asked Josh as I hung up the phone.

"Sure," he said enthusiastically. Then he added—more calmly and seriously—"I mean, I can see you need some help here with the new dog and all. I guess I could stay a while longer and help. But I have to check with Father Tierney."

Josh was waiting for Father Tierney to answer the phone when he put his hand over the mouthpiece and told me,

"You'll have to pretend you're your mom. He'll never let me stay otherwise."

A minute later I was telling a priest that I was Jan O'Connell and could Josh Greene stay for dinner.

And I got away with it.

I'm a pretty good cook. I made hamburgers and heated up some leftover spaghetti while Josh read to me from the "You and Your Puppy" pamphlet.

This is what we learned about housebreaking a puppy: It's hard.

We decided the best thing was to spread newspapers all over the kitchen floor and keep No-Name in there. We went into the living room to watch the movie channel on cable. I sat in my dad's old chair, which George thinks is his chair now, and that I know is my chair. Josh sat on the couch.

This is what was on: *Frankenstein*. This is what Josh and I both like a lot: horror movies.

When *Frankenstein* was over and before *Bride of Frankenstein* began I asked Josh, "Do you know how to cook popcorn in a microwave oven?"

"Put it in a pot and stick it in the oven, I guess."

"You put the popcorn in a paper bag," I explained. "And close it tight. Then you know what happens?"

"Guess I don't," he answered.

I got up. "Come on, I'll show you."

"Can't," he said as he stood up. "I gotta get back to St. Joe's."

I didn't feel like being alone, so I said, "Maybe you should just stay over."

"Sure!" he said. "That's a great idea." Then he added, "I mean, so you won't be alone if it takes all night for the baby to come and everything." It was pretty clear that Josh was more excited about the baby than I was. "But we have to call Father Tierney again," he said.

"And I get to tell him?" I asked.

27

"Right."

So we called Father Tierney.

"You're sure now, Mrs. O'Connell?" Father said after I told him how *we* wanted Josh to stay over. "It won't be too much trouble?"

"Not at all, Father," I answered in my most grown-up voice. "Josh is a fine young man. It would be a pleasure to have him stay with us." Then I added for good measure, "I'm helping him and Aviva with their history homework."

Josh was doubling over with laughter.

"Well, that's very kind of you, Mrs. O'Connell. We like our boys to be in normal family environments whenever possible. It's very kind of you. God bless you."

"And you, too," I answered. "Good night, Father."

When I hung up the phone I hooted with laughter. Tears were running down my face. I stuck the bag of popcorn in the microwave, put on the timer, and watched Josh's face as the bag started to jump with the pops of corn. No-Name barked for the first time since I'd met him and Josh and I had a great time in our "normal family environment."

When *Bride of Frankenstein* was over and *Frankenstein Meets the Wolfman* had just started, the phone rang again.

I answered it.

"He's here, Aviva!" George shouted on the other end. "A beautiful little boy. Perfect."

"Great," I said as enthusiastically as I could.

"As soon as they bring your mom up to her room I'll come and get you so you can see him before he's even an hour old."

"That's all right," I said. "I'll wait until tomorrow. You stay with Mom."

"You sure?" he said. "It's no trouble."

"I'm sure," I said. I checked my watch. Twelve o'clock. "It's real late."

"Yeah, I guess it is. Well, tomorrow then. I'll be home in a while. But I guess you'll be sleeping."

"Right," I said. "Oh, and Josh too. He's staying over. Father Tierney said it was okay."

"That's terrific," he said. "Hey, let me talk to him."

This is the thing about Josh and George: They're friends. Josh likes George much more than I do. Maybe that's because Josh doesn't have anybody, so he's not too fussy.

While Josh asked George all sorts of questions about the baby—how big he was, whether he cried yet, and how my mom felt—I got sheets and stuff for the couch out of the linen closet. Then I went into the kitchen to throw away the newspapers and pick up my puppy. This is where he was sleeping: under the kitchen table in Mop's old spot.

When I came into the living room with No-Name, Josh was putting the sheet on the couch. Suddenly I was very tired, plus sick to my stomach from so much popcorn and soda.

"Do I have to put newspapers on my bedroom floor?" I asked Josh as No-Name and I headed for my room.

Josh seemed pretty tired, too. "Nah," he said. "I wouldn't let him sleep in my bed though. I mean, you never know."

"Good thinking," I answered. "Night."

"Night," Josh answered as he turned the TV off on *Frankenstein Meets the Wolfman.*

When I was getting into my nightgown I remembered I hadn't offered Josh a pair of George's pajamas to wear to bed. Would he sleep in his clothes? And wear them to school the next day?

In the morning I woke up to wet licks on my right hand. "Mornin' Mop," I mumbled. *Mop?* I opened my eyes and

29

looked at my hand hanging toward the floor. Not Mop. No-Name.

"Mornin', puppy," I said as I picked him up and raised him over my head. He wiggled his tail and tried to lick my hands some more.

Then I remembered Josh had stayed over and Mom and George had their baby. I got up and dressed. Then No-Name and I went into the kitchen.

This was my situation that Thursday morning: I had to feed the dog, take care of my company—Josh—and make sure that he and I went to school separately. No way was *anyone* going to know that Josh Greene stayed over at my house. On top of all that, I hadn't done my homework.

Josh and George were in the kitchen. George was cooking up a storm. Bacon, pancakes—the works. Josh was all cleaned up and had on one of George's blue denim shirts. The only other time I'd ever seen Josh Greene in a shirt with a collar on it was at his grandmother's funeral.

"Hi," I said as I came into the room.

"Hiya," Josh said through a mouthful of bacon.

"Mornin', big sister," George answered as he turned around and saluted me with his spatula. He had on a grin two times the size of his face . . . until he saw No-Name. Then it changed into a big question mark.

"This is my new dog," I said. I put him on the floor and went to the cupboard for his dog food. "I haven't named him yet. Isn't he cute? Josh gave him to me."

"Josh?"

"I guess you could say I did," Josh said proudly.

George flipped the pancakes and bent down to take a look at No-Name. "He is cute," he said as he rubbed his hand through the pup's hair. "But, Aviva, a new baby and a new pup at the same time? It would have been better if you'd talked it over with your mother and me."

"He's my dog," I said. "I'll take care of him. And he'll

go with me to Dad's—I mean Miriam's. He won't bother you at all."

The pancakes were burning. George scraped them into the basket and poured some fresh batter into the pan. He didn't sound so happy when he said, "Do me a favor, Aviva. Don't tell your mother about the puppy for a day or so."

"Why?" I asked.

"Because," he said without turning from the stove, "I said so."

This was the first time George O'Connell ever spoke to me like he was my father or something. I was speechless.

Josh didn't pay any attention. He was too busy gobbling down his breakfast.

When George came over to put pancakes on my plate and more on Josh's, he changed the subject. "I think you should take the day off from school and celebrate your new brother. Your mom would love to see you this morning."

Josh ate his pancakes. No-Name ate his dog food. George poured more batter onto the griddle. "I have a lot to do at school today," I said to his back. "Eighth grade is a very important year. I can't afford to miss even one day."

"I see," George said. "And just when do you intend to go over there?" He looked real tired when he came back to the table with his own breakfast. I knew I was being a brat to ruin his first day of having a baby.

"I'll go right after school," I said in a nicer voice. "If that's all right."

George smiled at me. "It'll be all right." He took a bite of his pancake. He had back his new-father good cheer. "He's really beautiful, Aviva. We just want you to see him as soon as possible." He patted Josh on the shoulder. "You too, Josh. You'll come by as soon as Jan and the baby get home."

"Great," Josh said.

Suddenly a bad, bathroom smell took over the bacon-and-pancake smells in the kitchen. No-Name.

"Sorry," I said to both of them as I went for paper towels to clean up after *my* dog. At least it wasn't on a rug, I consoled myself.

"Don't forget," George said as he opened a window to let the bad air out and some fresh air in. "Not a word to your mom about the puppy. Give her a day or two."

"Bad dog," I scolded No-Name. "Bad dog." But I had a feeling No-Name didn't understand what I was trying to tell him, because he was already on the other side of the room, chewing the laces on Josh's sneakers.

After school I went home for a few minutes to check on No-Name. I put him in the backyard, but he didn't connect outside with going to the bathroom. Besides, he'd done enough indoors for three dogs! I cleaned up all that and checked on Myrtle who was sleeping under my bed. Turtles are a lot easier to take care of than puppies. Then I spread clean papers all over the kitchen floor and put out fresh food and water.

Afterward I ate two tablespoons of Marshmallow Fluff and I took the bus to Mary Fletcher Hospital.

The only time I was in the hospital before was when Sister Bernard Marie brought our sixth-grade class there to sing Christmas carols. It was different coming to visit your own mother.

When I got inside I went over to the desk that said RE-CEPTION. ALL VISITORS STOP HERE.

"Can I help you?" a young man asked.

I told him my mother's name and he gave me an orange card that said VISITOR, ROOM 410.

I took the elevator to the fourth floor with two nurses and a doctor. I walked down the long corridor until I found room 410. The door was opened. My mother was half-sitting in this real narrow bed. She had on a nightgown I'd never seen with little daisies all over it, and a pink ribbon holding her hair back in a bow. The room was filled with flowers. Was I supposed to bring a present?

She looked at me standing in the doorway and smiled the kind of smile that's almost crying the person is so happy. "There you are," she exclaimed. "Oh, Aviva. Come give me a kiss." She held her arms open. I went over and bent down and gave her a kiss on the forehead.

"Hi, Mom," I said. "Guess what I got?"

"A baby brother," she answered as she squeezed my hand.

"Besides that," I said.

"Did George give you a present?"

"Josh gave it to me," I said. "He gave me a puppy." I got all excited just thinking about my puppy. "Wait'll you see him, Mom. He's so cute."

"A puppy," she said quietly. "Well, what a surprise." She said it like it wasn't a good one.

Before I could tell Mom any more about No-Name a nurse came into the room. "This must be Aviva," she said when she saw me. She had a baby in her arms.

"Aviva," my mom said, "this is Miss Gonzalez."

"Nice to meet you," I said to Miss Gonzalez with the baby in her arms.

"Meet your new brother," she said as she walked right over to me and stuck this baby under my nose. This is what he looked like: His skin was all splotchy. His eyes weren't open and he had this scrunched-up look—like a Cabbage Patch Kid. I mean, Cabbage Patch Kids are cute and all, but you wouldn't want to wake up one day looking like one.

The nurse and Mom were smiling at me, waiting for me to say something nice.

"What's his name?" I asked.

33

Baby squiggled in the nurse's arms and started to cry, which made him look uglier than ever.

"I think we can try nursing him," the nurse said to my mother as she took the baby over to my mother and handed him to her.

"Oh, my beautiful baby," my mother said. She took him in her arms and started to breast-feed him. I thought it was a pretty disgusting thing to be doing in front of the nurse and everything.

"Come sit next to me," my mom said.

I sat at the bottom of the bed and tried not to look at her and her baby.

"His name," she said in this cooing voice—like she was telling the baby, not me—"His name is John Edward Linton O'Connell. 'John,' after George's father; 'Edward,' after your grandfather; 'Linton,' my maiden name; 'O'Connell,' which is his last name." She looked up at me. "What do you think? Do you like it?"

"It's awfully long," I said. "I mean that's a lot to write on the heading of a test at school or something."

My mom shifted the baby to her other breast and laughed. "He'll just use the first and last name on papers and things. We'll call him 'John' or 'Johnny.' "

John Edward Linton O'Connell wasn't interested in any more food. "Honey," my mother said to me as she winced and shifted around in the bed. "Could you take him while I get more comfortable?" She held John Edward Linton O'Connell out for me without even waiting for me to say yes or no.

I took him. I'd never held such a small person before. It felt like he didn't weigh anything!

"I'm going to call him 'Jelo,' " I told my mother.

"Jello?" She was lying down now, on her side. There was no way she could hold the baby, so I just laid him next to her.

"Yeah," I explained. "Those are his initials. J-E-L-O."

She was touching him all over. Rubbing his belly and head, counting his little fingers, and talking to him in this soft, silly voice. "Jelo. That's a funny name. Our little Jelo."

"I've got to think of a name for my dog, too," I said.

"Why don't you name him Pudding?" she said with a mischievous grin.

"Very funny," I said. "I've been thinking about 'Willie.' "

"After Grandpa Granger?" she asked.

"Exactly," I told her.

"I see," she said. But she didn't say whether she thought it was a good idea. Since Grandpa Granger had died when I was little, I figured it would make my dad feel good and everything.

"So, how are we doing in here?" Nurse Gonzalez asked as she rustled back into the room. She walked right over to look at the baby. "He's a handsome fellow, isn't he?" she said to my mother and me. My mother agreed, but I didn't say anything. "Well let's go, handsome fellow," Miss Gonzalez said to Jelo as she picked him up. "Do you need anything else right now?" she asked my mother.

My mother smiled up at her. "I'm fine," she said as she slid deeper under the covers. "Just tired."

The nurse looked at me when she said, "Maybe Mommy needs to take a nap." Which meant she thought I should go.

After she left I stood up. "I guess I'll go."

"Please don't," my mother said as she reached for me. "You just got here."

"That nurse said you have to sleep," I explained.

She shifted over to one side of the little bed and patted the space where Jelo had been lying.

"Honey," she said. "You look pretty tired too. Why

35

don't you just lie down here. We'll both take a nap. Just take your shoes off."

"I dunno," I said. "Willie's alone and everything."

"Just for a little while," she said.

So I did. I took off my shoes and got into bed with my mom. We were face to face. "Close your eyes," she said. When I did she rubbed my hairline right above my ear the way she always did when I was little and couldn't fall asleep.

"You know what I've been thinking about today?" she asked.

"How happy you are to have a baby?" I said without opening my eyes.

"Yes, of course. But I've also been remembering the day you were born. It was the happiest day of my life, Aviva. You were so cute and scrawny and had all this black hair on your head. The nurse—I even remember her name—Mrs. Delorme. Well, Mrs. Delorme tied the hair on the top of your head with a little pink ribbon." My mom was talking soft and rubbing my ear all the time she was telling me. I don't know what else she said because I fell asleep.

The next thing I heard was George saying, "Shhh, she's asleep." And a woman saying, "This must all be pretty exciting for her."

I opened my eyes and looked at *four* faces. George, George's mother, George's father and George's grown-up daughter, Cynthia.

Everyone smiled at me and said hello.

I was all cramped from sleeping in such a tiny spot. "Hello," I answered. I got up and looked under the bed for my shoes.

"So," George's father said as he held out a big green bottle. "Champagne for my namesake."

"And roses," Mrs. O'Connell said as she held out a dozen roses to my mother.

"And," Cynthia said, "a teddy bear." She put this most perfect, brown teddy bear with big plaid ribbon next to Mom where I'd been sleeping.

"My goodness," Mom said as she inspected the teddy. "Lucky baby!" She held it out for me to see. "Look, Aviva. Isn't it adorable?"

"Yeah," I said.

"We saw that lucky baby in the nursery on the way in," Mrs. O'Connell said. "So beautiful." She put her arm around George. "Already looks like his daddy."

George looked at Cynthia. "Like Cynthia when she was a baby too. Don't you think, Mother?"

"Well, yes, but that's because Cynthia looked so much like you, dear."

I decided not to tell them I thought the baby looked like a Cabbage Patch Kid. "Well, bye everybody," I said with a little wave. "I've got to go."

"Don't go," George said. "Stay. Then we'll all go have Italian at Stangoni's."

"Can't," I said. "I've got things to do at home. Homework and stuff. Thanks anyway."

My mom tried to get me to go with them. Cindy tried to get me to go with them. But I wouldn't. I didn't want to be with all those people.

"Bye, Mom," I said as I bent over to give her a kiss goodbye.

"I'll call you later," she said with a sort of sad smile.

And I left.

The first thing I did when I got home was play with Willie. I told him how much I loved him and that he would grow up to be strong and wise like Mop. Then I made my supper—two peanut butter and Fluff sandwiches. I was eating them and thinking about how lonely it would be to live alone when the phone rang. It was my dad.

He knew all about Mom's new baby and my new puppy. I told him I thought Jelo was ugly, but Dad wasn't very interested in the baby. What he mostly called to say was that since Mom was in the hospital and everything, why didn't I go to his place—Miriam's place—for the rest of the week.

"Then," he said, "if you want to go back to Mom's on Monday to be there when she gets home from the hospital, we can adjust your schedule."

"The day Mom comes home George's mother is coming for a whole week," I told my dad. "She's going to help with the baby and sleep in my room. So if it's all right I'll go to Miriam's tomorrow and stay until Mom's next turn."

"Why don't I come and get you right now?" my dad suggested. "We'll throw some more spaghetti in the pot. Okay?"

Peanut butter and Marshmallow Fluff sat in a gooey blob in the pit of my stomach. I had a ton of homework. And my room was a mess.

"How about tomorrow," I said. "I already ate."

"If that's what you want," he said. "It's probably better at this end, too. Gives me a chance to tell Miriam all about that puppy of yours."

I looked around the room for Willie. He was chewing on the edge of a cabinet.

"Dad," I asked. "When we got Mop he was all housebroken and everything, wasn't he?"

Dad laughed. "Hardly! You were so little yourself, I guess you don't remember. Aviva, the first year with a puppy is very hard work. But don't worry, honey, I'll help you."

After I hung up I pulled Willie away from the cabinet and saw the damage he'd done to that door in just a few minutes.

Help couldn't come soon enough.

* * *

When I got to school the next day I found this note on my desk.

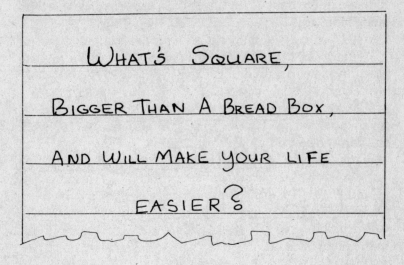

WHAT'S SQUARE,

BIGGER THAN A BREAD BOX,

AND WILL MAKE YOUR LIFE

EASIER?

I wrote back:

a refridgerator for
my bedroom!

I handed it to Josh. He read my answer, looked straight ahead like he was listening to Mrs. P.P. and shook his head "No."

Between Math and History he passed the note back to me with another clue:

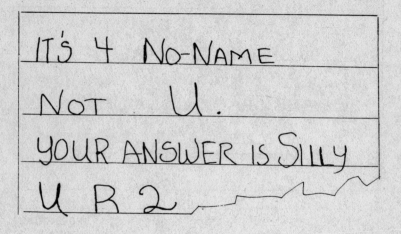

IT'S 4 NO-NAME
NOT U.
YOUR ANSWER IS SILLY
U R 2

I wrote back:

This game is silly
And his name is
Willie!

40

Before lunch Josh handed it back.

THIS ISN'T A GAME

IT'S A PRESENT

4 NO-NAME !

The bell rang for lunch before I had time to write another guess. "So what is it?" I asked Josh as I followed him out of the room.

"A crate," he answered. "Like that wire thing he was in at Angelo's. Angelo's giving you one. For free. He told me all about how to use it to housebreak No-Name."

"You mean he does it in that thing?" I asked as we headed down the hall toward the lunch room. "Like it's a bathroom or something?"

"No," Josh explained. "Just the opposite. The crate is his home, so he won't mess it up. You keep him in there except when you're playing with him or walking him. That's how he learns to go outside."

"That's awful," I said. "It's like a jail."

"Not to the dog it's not," he answered. "To No-Name it'll be home."

"*Willie*," I said as we walked into the cafeteria. "His name is *Willie*."

"*No-Name*," Josh answered.

"*Willie*," I said firmly.

41

"Hey, Aviva," Louise called to me from our usual table. My friends were all sitting there watching me talk to Josh Greene.

Josh said real loud, so everyone around would hear and not think we were girlfriend and boyfriend or anything: "Aviva, you're crazy."

"Not as crazy as you are, Josh Greene," I shouted back.

"What was that all about?" Rita asked me when I sat down with my lunch.

"What was what all about?" I asked back as I took out my tuna fish sandwich.

"Don't play dumb, Aviva. You know. With you and Josh."

"I thought you had a crush on Bob Hanley," Louise added. "I hope you're not going to settle for Josh."

"Me and Josh Greene?" I said. "Give me a break."

"Who can go to the movies Saturday night?" Sue asked to change the subject. I guess you could say Sue was my only best friend in that group.

We'd all decided that if we wanted to get in with the high school kids we had to start going out on Saturday nights— even if we didn't have boyfriends. We'd just sort of hang out. Go to a movie, go for pizza, walk up and down Main Street. Saturday was the first night we were putting this plan into action. Rita, Louise, Janet, Sue, and me.

We had this agreement. If any of us got picked up by a guy—like, say, Bob Hanley wanted to walk me home or something—well, then we'd always make sure that there were two girls left. We promised never to leave one of us out alone, looking like she didn't have any friends or anything.

For the rest of the lunch hour we planned what to wear on Saturday night, and how they would help me get Bob Hanley to notice me and forget about Joanne Richards. No one bugged me again about Josh Greene.

CHAPTER FOUR

SEPTEMBER			OCTOBER			
DAD	DAD	DAD	DAD	DAD	DAD	DAD
28 M	29 T	30 W	1 T	2 F	3 S	4 S

OUR STUFF LOOKED DIFFERENT IN MIRIAM'S PLACE from the way it looked in my dad's and my apartment.

First of all there were dainty, flower-patterned pillows all over the couch. And the outdoor table and chairs we'd used for a dining-room set were outdoors on the terrace. There was a red chrysanthemum plant in the middle of the table. Mostly there was Miriam. I hated sharing my dad with her.

This is what Miriam was that I wasn't: very feminine and pretty. She was also the neatest—meaning cleanest—person I'd ever met. This is what you had to do if you lived with Miriam: take off your shoes at the front door and put on "indoor" shoes. She said the Japanese do it all the time and it keeps the floors "clean enough to eat off."

This is how Miriam looked when she first saw Willie: disappointed.

This is what she said: "Well now, isn't that a cute puppy." She added, hopefully, "Will he stay in that nice cage all the time?"

"It's not a cage," I told her. "It's a crate. Until he gets bigger he'll stay in there a lot."

"Bigger?" she said.

"He's a terrier," my dad explained. "He won't get too big, honey." Dad calls Miriam "honey," too, I thought, as I watched him mark off below his knee with his hand to show how high Willie would get.

I wondered if Willie would have to have indoor shoes, too.

Miriam has some good points. One of them is that she's

43

a terrific cook. That night we had stuffed roasted chicken and salad. There were lit candles and fresh flowers on the table. I had my apple juice in a wine glass and Miriam made a toast. "To Aviva," she said as she smiled at Dad and me. "And, of course, Willie. Happy days at 39 Heath Avenue." That was her address.

During dinner Dad told me all about how he and Mom had housebroken Mop. He said it should be easier with Willie because of using the crate.

Miriam asked me how it felt to have a baby brother. I told her that Jelo was sort of funny looking but that my mom was happy with him anyway.

Dad said how great it was when I was born. "You were pretty scrawny," he said. "But you had this incredible black hair. The nurse, I even remember her name, Mrs. Delmonte. She tied your hair in a ribbon."

" 'Delorme,' " I corrected him. "Her name was 'Delorme.' Mom told me. It was a pink ribbon."

"Jan told you?" Dad said.

"Uh-huh," I answered. "When I visited her in the hospital."

Dad had this warm, sweet smile, like he was remembering a happy time. He told some more stuff about when I was born, including how it rained the day they brought me home from the hospital.

Miriam was pretty bored.

After dinner Dad and I walked Willie. He loved being outdoors. This little puff of blond fur sniffed at the grass, pulled on the leash to chase a squirrel, wasn't frightened by the roar of passing cars, and did what he was supposed to do outside.

When we got back inside Miriam had done all the dishes. I went to my room with Willie and put him back in his crate while I did my homework. He whimpered to get out. I went to my bureau and found the little red sneaker that Mop had loved to chew on and gave it to Willie. He sniffed at it curiously. "It's yours now," I told him. "Mop would want you to have it."

He curled up in a corner of the crate, put his little paws on the sneaker, and started to chew.

Miriam and Dad were talking in low, angry voices in the living room. I went to my door to hear what they were fighting about. The only thing I understood was when Miriam said, "If you had such a wonderful time with Jan, why'd you leave her?" And Dad saying, "Don't be ridiculous, Miriam. Of course we were happy when we had a baby. That was then. This is now."

I listened a little longer until I heard normal talking tones, like the fight was over.

As I sat down to try to catch up on my history assignment, I thought they wouldn't have had a fight if I'd stayed at Mom's. Then I thought maybe Dad won't like living with Miriam. Maybe he and Miriam will even stop loving each other and Dad and I can get our own apartment again.

Saturday was the weekend of Fall Festival. That meant all the stores would be open on Saturday until nine o'clock. So Sue and I met Rita, Janet, and Louise at the mall to walk around and stuff before we went to the movies.

This is what the mall is like: It's under Main Street. What you do is get on an escalator at the street level and ride it down into the mall which is like an indoor village with streets and shops. It's terrific in the winter because even the streets are heated and you can go from store to store with your coat off. And it's terrific in the summer because it's air-conditioned. That night I would have rather stayed on ground level, walking on Main Street, because it was a beautiful evening—warm and clear. But everyone said that the high school kids would probably be hanging out in Go for the Gold, the record shop, and since we were out because we wanted to be seen, we'd better go there.

Louise, Rita, and Janet walked a few steps ahead of Sue and me. To get to Go for the Gold we had to pass Miriam's Magic.

Here's the truth. I'd only been in Miriam's store once—when it opened and she had a party. It's a nice store with the sort of clothes my friends would like that are too expensive for my mom and me to buy.

Here's another truth. Sue was the only one of my friends who knew that Dad and I not only knew Miriam, but that we lived with her.

Louise turned to me from staring at the clothes in Miriam's window. "Aviva, your father's in there. Selling things!"

"I know," I said. "Miriam's his girlfriend. He's helping out for the Fall Festival."

Sue and I looked in the window, too. There was Dad, all smiles, wrapping a dress in purple tissue paper and chatting with a customer.

"She's his girlfriend?" Rita said. "Why didn't you tell us? It's like the *best* store. Let's go in. Maybe she'll give us a discount."

Before I could say anything they'd marched into Miriam's Magic, with Sue and me pulling up the rear.

The store looked great, with bright, fresh-looking clothes hanging on the racks and piled high on a natural-colored wicker table and a shiny black lacquered bureau. And there was a couch for people to sit on while their wives and friends tried on clothes. For the Festival, Miriam had put a big punch bowl of cider and baskets of donuts on the coffee table in front of the couch.

Dad was doing his customer's credit-card slip and Miriam was taking a sweater off the wicker table and holding it up to show a young woman. It was two shades of red and the most beautiful sweater I'd ever seen. "It'll look great on you," Miriam was saying. That girl was so pretty anything would have looked great on her. Miriam saw us before my dad did. "Aviva," she exclaimed. "I'm so glad you decided to drop by after all." Louise and Rita gave me a you've-been-holding-back-on-us look.

"Hi," I said. "The store looks nice."

"Hi, honey," my dad called over his shoulder as he went over to help a customer who was looking at the pile of bright-colored socks on the bureau. I could tell he was having a good time. I guess helping someone buy clothes is more fun than correcting college history papers.

Miriam left her customer to come over to us. "And you brought your friends," she said to me.

I introduced everybody and "my friends" oohed and ahhed over the clothes in her store. Louise even asked for a job. "Well," Miriam said as she put her arm around my shoulders. "I guess I'll be needing extra help at Christmas time but my roommate here has first dibbs on a job." I got another one of those you've-been-holding-out-on-us looks from Louise.

Just then the pretty woman called to Miriam, "What do you think?" She had on the red sweater and was turning this way and that in front of the full-length mirror. Everyone, including my dad and his customer, said that it was perfect on her, especially because of her dark hair. The girl loved it too, and said she'd take it. Dad left the lady with the socks and went to the cash register to take her money. Then Miriam looked at me with this big smile and said, "You know who else would look great in that sweater?"

"Who?" I asked.

"You," she said. There was only one more like it in that pile on the table. Miriam handed it to me.

"She's right, Aviva," Rita said. "Try it on."

I took off my old sweater and put it on over my shirt. Then

I looked in the mirror. Everyone oohed and ahhed the way they did for the college girl. Then Miriam said the most amazing thing. She said, "It's yours. A present from me."

I couldn't believe it. I'd never had such a beautiful sweater! My dad was happy too. He said thank you to Miriam before I caught my breath. I gave her a little hug and said, "Thank you. It's wonderful. I'm so happy." And I meant it. I did feel really happy but I also felt a little weird, like maybe Miriam gave me the sweater because she wanted me to like her.

My friends couldn't believe how lucky I was, and after we left the store, all five of us walked in a row instead of Sue and me walking behind.

"Maybe she'll need more than one person to work for the holidays," Louise said. "I mean it's getting to be a very popular store and she has such nice things."

"Maybe," I said. And I gave Sue a nudge and smile that said, If Miriam needs more than one person you've got the job, because you're my best, most loyal friend.

We went up the escalator and walked to the movie theater. I was glad it was a warm night so I didn't have to cover my new sweater with a jacket or anything.

This is where we sat in the movie theater: four rows behind a bunch of high school kids who'd graduated from St. Agnes the June before. Louise said, "Hi, guys," when one of them turned around to see who was in the theater. Then all of them turned around to see who'd said "Hi," and they said "Hi" back to Louise, and "How's the old dump?" (meaning St. Agnes). That's when Josh Greene and Ronnie Cioffi came down the aisle, saying, "Hey, Hey," and "How's it going?" and sat right up front with them.

As soon as the theater darkened for the movie to begin, Rita, who was on the other side of Sue, said I should change places with her. I figured it was because she was short and couldn't see or something. When I got to my new place Sue pointed directly in front of me.

Four seats up. Bob Hanley. I stared at the back of his head and thought about how much I liked him. Good-looking, taller than me, a great athlete, and he made my heart pound. It *must* be love, I thought. He was the last one in his row, but not in the last seat. There were four empty seats next to him. If we'd gone in that row, I thought, with Louise being so friendly with all those kids, then maybe I'd have sat next to him. Josh was in our class and *he* was sitting with them.

I imagined what it would be like. As I sat down I'd give him a big smile and say, "Hi. How's it going?" And he'd say, "Hi. It's great to see you. What a terrific sweater." Then when the lights went down and the movie began, he'd drape his arm around the back of my seat. I was thinking about whether he'd kiss me when two high school girls came in and sat in that row. Joanne Richards took "my" seat next to Bob Hanley. It was pretty hard to imagine Bob Hanley putting his arm around my shoulder and kissing me when that was exactly what he was doing with Joanne Richards four rows in front of me.

So I tried to watch the movie, but I can't even remember what it was called or what it was about, only that Bob kept his arm around Joanne's shoulder for the whole movie, and I supposed they were holding hands too.

About halfway through the movie this beeping noise came from that row. Everyone turned to Josh and said, "Hey, shut that thing off." And "Sh-hh." And "Turkey, keep it down."

The noise stopped and Josh got up and ran out of the theater.

I thought about that for a while. Did Josh think he was making a joke with an alarm or something? Did the high school kids hurt his feelings by not laughing? I was surprised at Josh. I figured that the risk you take when you play a practical joke is some people won't think it's funny. But I was surprised that Josh was so touchy. Maybe living in an orphanage was getting him down. Cioffi should have gone after him or something was what I thought. I knew I would have if I were a boy and his friend instead of being a girl and his friend.

When the movie was finally over and the lights went on and we all stood up, Louise sent the message down our little group that we should take our time getting out of the theater so we'd come out at the same time as the high school kids. Which meant I left our row as Joanne Richards and Bob Hanley came up the aisle hand in hand. This is what I hated: walking behind them.

Josh Greene was waiting on the street. "Where'd you go, man?" Bob asked him.

Josh held up a beeper. "Emergency at my job," he said as we all stared at the little silver box.

"Yeah?" Bob said. "And they call you on that thing, like a doctor or something?"

"Right," Josh answered as he hung the beeper on his belt.

"So what was the emergency?" Louise asked.

Josh Greene looked at me when he quietly said, "A dog was hit by a car."

"Oh," said Joanne sadly. "Did he . . . ?"

"No," Josh interrupted her. "We were able to save her. She'll be all right."

"That's incredible!" Bob said. "You saved a life."

I tried not to think about my dog Mop and how he couldn't be saved when he got hit by a car. Instead I thought about Bob. He really appreciates what Angelo and Josh do, I thought. I learned something new about Bob Hanley tonight. He's sensitive and loves animals. No wonder I have a crush on him. He's absolutely perfect. The problem was it looked like Joanne Richards thought so, too.

Everyone headed for Sammy's Pizza. By then there were about fifteen of us. As we walked along, our group of five got slowly pushed to the back. So by the time we got to Sammy's it was Bob and Joanne and Josh and Ronnie and a couple of the other freshman guys who went in first. Then the rest of the high school kids.

When it was clear they were all going in together, Louise said, "Slow down. Let's stay here for a second and check things out. That way we can play our strategy and not go in there like jerks. If we don't plan, we'll end up just sitting with one another." So we stood in front of Sammy's, like we were so involved in conversation that we hadn't bothered to go in yet. Janet looked through the window while the rest of us made sure we didn't.

"They're in two big booths," she reported. "But there's room for at least two more in each booth."

"Who's Greene sitting with?" Louise asked.

"Bob, Joanne, Ronnie, Frank, and Stephen," Janet answered.

"Then David's in the other booth," Louise concluded. David was Louise's heartthrob. She thought for a second, then said, "This is what we do. Aviva, you know Josh and you're interested in Bob. So you and Sue go over to that booth and say something to Josh about the dog he saved. You know, because you both like animals and everything. Then you'll sit down. The rest of us," she looked around at Rita and Janet, "will sit at the other table."

No way am I doing this, I thought. Bob is sitting with Joanne and I'm not going to remind Josh about Mop and the accident. No way.

"Okay," Louise said, without waiting to see if Sue and I had agreed. "Let's go." She pushed through the door. Rita

51

and Janet followed her. I could see them smiling and hear them being friendly, all "Hi's" and everything.

"I dunno," Sue said as she looked at me to see what I thought about going in there.

"I know," I said. "I'm not doing it."

She smiled at me. "Good. Let's just go home."

As we walked away, I took one last look at Sammy's. Louise was sitting right next to David.

I felt sort of down. Then I got this idea. "Want to stay over at Miriam's with me?" I asked Sue. "I'm sure she won't mind. She and my dad probably aren't home yet anyway. You can see my new dog."

Sue loved the idea. We went right to Miriam's and called Sue's mom who said, "Sure. Just be a good girl."

Then we took Willie out of his crate and walked him. When we were back inside we let him play on the kitchen floor while we ate and ate and ate. Leftover lasagna right from the fridge, peanut butter and Fluff sandwiches, ice cream, and a whole quart of apple juice. When we were finally full, Dad called to see if I was home and to say they'd be out for another hour, because he and Miriam were relaxing over a late dinner.

Sue and I put Willie in his crate and went into Miriam's and my dad's room. We opened Miriam's closet door to see her clothes. A huge closet packed full! And all of it was beautiful.

"You're so lucky," Sue said as she felt the silk on a whole row of blouses in different colors. "I bet she'll lend you stuff and everything. She really likes you."

I looked down at my wonderful new sweater. Maybe living with Miriam wouldn't be so bad after all.

CHAPTER FIVE

OCTOBER

Mom	Mom	Mom	Mom	Mom	Mom	Mom
5 M	6 T	7 W	8 T	9 F	10 S	11 S

WHEN I GOT TO MOM'S AFTER SCHOOL ON MONDAY the whole house was upside down.

First of all I practically tripped over my mother and Willie. My mom was on her hands and knees picking up a mess Willie had made on the floor and he was nibbling the heel of her sneaker. Her baby was in the living room crying up a storm.

She looked up at me. "You finish cleaning this up," she said as she handed me the roll of paper towels, "and I'll get the baby. Here, help me up, will you?" She put out her hand. I took it and gave her a pull up. "I'm still pretty sore," she explained, "from the delivery."

She looked like my old mom again. No more beachball belly. Only she didn't even say, "Hello, how are you?" like she used to. Just, "Boy, Aviva, a baby and a puppy are quite a handful. We've got to work out a system here."

"Boy, Willie," I told my puppy as I cleaned up his stinky mess. "We better tell her about using the crate."

After I finished with the floor I opened the cupboard to get a hit of Marshmallow Fluff. There wasn't any. I went to the refrigerator for some apple juice. There wasn't any.

"Boy, Mom," I said as I carried Willie into the living room. "There isn't any food in the house. Didn't you shop or anything?"

Mom was walking back and forth on this puke-green rug that used to be in George's apartment. The baby was still wailing. "George is doing the shopping after work," she

53

said. "Fluff and juice are on the list." She gave me a weak, tired smile. "Hi, sweetie. How are you?"

"I'm okay," I said. But I didn't tell her about going out Saturday or about the sweater Miriam gave me or how I had a crush on Bob Hanley. Instead I asked her, "Why didn't you keep Willie in the crate? Didn't Dad tell you?"

"He told me," she said as she sat down on the couch. Jelo had stopped crying and was hanging over her shoulder. "Come look at your brother's face," she said. "He doesn't cry all the time, you know."

I went around the couch to look at his face. It looked the same as in the hospital. Only now his eyes were opened. He looked in my direction, but I knew he couldn't really see me. I mean he was too little and everything.

"Hi, Jelo," I said.

I sat next to my mom and put Willie on my lap. I told Mom how to use Willie's crate. She said she'd tried keeping him in it, but he whined and fussed so to get out that Jelo was crying all the time. So she let Willie out so Jelo would sleep. But that was a problem, too, because Willie kept getting underfoot. Which, she explained, could be really dangerous when she was carrying Jelo around. The other problem was that Willie was going to the bathroom all over the house.

I looked at Willie fast asleep on my lap. "He didn't mind staying in the crate at Dad's, I mean Miriam's," I told her.

Mom shifted Jelo off her shoulder and cradled him in her arms. He was asleep, too.

"Hmm," she said. "Maybe it's because this place is new to him and you weren't here."

"He was here before," I answered.

"But so were you. Today you weren't."

"I dunno," I said. "I thought he was trained and everything."

She sighed. "It takes more than a week, Aviva," she said

as she ran her free hand over Willie's soft fur. "He's awfully cute, but I do wish you'd asked me about it first. A
puppy and a new baby are a lot to take at once."

Yeah, I thought. I wish you'd asked me about having a
baby first too. I didn't tell her that though. I just said, "You
know, Mom, you probably shouldn't call Jelo my brother.
I mean he really isn't."

Then I went to my room, put Willie in his crate and did
some of my homework. I was there only a little while when
Mom knocked on my door. I thought, maybe she knows I
didn't have a snack or anything and is bringing me something to eat. "It's open," I said.

Mom came into my room and looked at Willie sleeping in
the crate. "If he'll stay in there and not make a fuss I guess
we can manage. Thank goodness you're old enough to
housebreak him yourself."

Then she told me Jelo was sleeping and I should leave my
door open so I'd hear him if he cried or anything. "I have
to get some sleep," she explained. "George and I were up
all night with the baby. It was much easier when I took you
home from the hospital." She sighed. "Or maybe I was just
younger."

Then she left.

I was tired too.

At dinner that night I started sneezing. And coughing. I
felt rotten. George said I was probably getting a cold. Mom
said I better not hold the baby.

As soon as dinner was over I walked Willie, put him in
his crate, and got ready for bed. My mom came in to check
on me. "You really feel sick, honey?" she asked.

"Yeah," I said. "I feel awful." And I did. She took my
temperature and I had a fever of 101.

"No school for you tomorrow," she said. She sort of
laughed, but not really, when she added, "A cranky baby,

55

a new puppy, and a sick daughter. Looks like I've got my hands full.''

She bent over my bed and kissed me on the forehead. ''Let's hope this bug doesn't go through the house.''

I went to sleep thinking about the house having a cold, blowing its window nose and coughing through its door mouth.

In the middle of the night Willie and I woke up to Jelo's crying. He stopped, but I couldn't go back to sleep. I just hoped with all my might that Willie didn't have to be walked. I lay there for a while, real still, to see if he'd stop rattling around in his crate and settle down again. Then, when the baby stopped crying, and Willie was quiet, I got up very quietly to go to the bathroom and get some water. My head was on fire. I felt woozy and weird. I didn't turn the light on in the hall or anything. But there was a light on in the living room. Mom and George and Jelo were on the couch together. George had his arm around Mom and Mom was nursing Jelo. They didn't see me. I just stood there watching them and listening to them coo and whisper over Jelo. George stroked his baby's head and gave my mom a kiss on the cheek. ''Thank you, honey,'' he said, ''for such a beautiful baby.''

I went back to bed and listened until they went back to their room before I went to the bathroom.

The next day I stayed in bed most of the time and watched TV. George walked Willie in the morning. Mom walked him in the afternoon.

Around four Mom brought me ginger ale, but first she took my temperature. It was back to normal, but I was still coughing and stuff so she said that I had to stay home at least one more day.

She sat on the edge of my bed. ''Would you like to come

out into the living room for the evening?'' she asked. ''You can watch TV there.''

''I'll stay here,'' I said.

Just then the doorbell rang. ''Who could that be?'' she asked, as if I would know.

She went to answer the door and I sat up in bed and listened.

''Josh!'' I heard her exclaim. ''How wonderful to see you. And a present! How sweet. Come on in and see the baby.''

The front door closed and they went into the living room together. Then I heard Josh say all the things people say about babies, like ''He's so little,'' and ''He's cute,'' and ''What tiny fingers,'' and ''Coochie-coochie-coo.''

Mom told Josh I was sick but getting better and would he like to stay for dinner. Josh said he had to go to work for two hours but could come back after that. ''I'll call St. Joseph's,'' she said, ''and ask Father Tierney's permission.''

Oh no, I thought. Father Tierney will hear the difference in our voices. He'll know that Josh and I set him up the night Jelo was born. ''Hey,'' Josh said to my mom. ''That'd be terrific. But maybe George should call when he gets home from work. I mean he knows Father Tierney and everything.''

My mom agreed and I started to breathe again. Josh Greene can be pretty clever.

After he left, I decided to take a shower and put on some real clothes. Maybe I'd go into the living room after all.

CHAPTER SIX

DAD	DAD	DAD	DAD	DAD	DAD	DAD
12 M	13 T	14 W	15 T	16 F	17 S	18 S

WAS I EVER GLAD TO GET BACK TO MIRIAM'S PLACE. I'd been sick almost the whole week I was at Mom's. Mom and George had been grumpy and tired because Jelo woke up crying about ten thousand times a night. And people kept coming by to see how cute he was. But except for the crying, Jelo just lay around doing nothing. Like Myrtle. I'd managed to keep the three basic rules that Sue had taught me about how to survive in a house with a baby.

Rule #1: When the baby cries, pretend you don't hear.

Rule #2: Never, ever, change a dirty diaper. If it's wet, maybe. If it's real dirty, call for help. Just say you don't do it, because once you do it's all over.

Rule #3: Have a book from school handy at all times. When they ask you to get the baby or the bottle or whatever, pick up your book and moan, "I've got so much homework. School's real hard this year."

It was pretty easy to keep these rules because I had a cold and no one wanted me to go near Jelo anyway.

Things were much more grown-up at Miriam's. Monday we went out together for Chinese food.

"So, Aviva," Dad said as he and I split the last of the chicken fried rice. "Have you started to plan your birthday party?"

My birthday is on Halloween and every year I have a combination birthday/Halloween party. My friends wear costumes and we eat pizza and then go trick-or-treating together. It's sort of a tradition. But last year no one wanted to wear costumes and we played kissing games instead of trick-or-treating. It wasn't even like it was Halloween or anything.

"I'm not having a party this year," I told my dad and Miriam.

Dad looked disappointed. He really likes family traditions and stuff like that. "Why on earth not?" he asked. "If Jan won't let you have it at the house because of the baby, you can have it at our place."

I looked at Miriam. "Sure," she said without blinking an eye. Twenty eighth graders partying in her beautiful apartment! Boy, I thought, she really must love my dad.

"It's not Mom who doesn't want it," I explained. "It's me. I've sort of outgrown it. Besides," I said, "there's a dance at the high school that Saturday and the eighth graders are invited." The other "besides," that I wasn't telling them, was that Bob Hanley would never come to my birthday party, but he would be at the dance.

"I see," Dad said. But you could tell he didn't.

Miriam understood though. One hundred percent. "Your first high school dance!" she exclaimed. "That's terrific. Now let's see, that's in two weeks so you'll be with us. Perfect." She pointed her chopsticks at my dad. "This is a big deal, Daddy," she said. "You're going to have to accept that your little girl is growing up." She turned back to me. "I think this dance is a great chance for you to present a new look. I'll make you over. New hairdo, new makeup, new outfit."

I couldn't believe she'd do that for me! "You will?" I said.

"Sure," she said. "It'll be my present."

"But you already gave me a sweater and . . ."

Dad interrupted me. "Make her over?" He looked at me in my navy sweatshirt, with no makeup, with my hair sticking out in all directions. "I like her just the way she is," he said.

You might like me just the way I am, Dad, I thought. But Bob Hanley doesn't. And even if Miriam's doing this to bribe me into liking her because she loves you, I'm going to take advantage of it.

"Every woman can use a perking up," Miriam said. "Woman," I thought. She's right. I am a woman now. A woman in love.

Miriam reached over and put her hand on top of mine and gave it a little squeeze. "It'll be great fun."

"Thank you," I told her, "for such a great present. I can't wait." As I squeezed her hand back I felt a little guilty for pretending I liked her, but I was already wondering: Will it work? Can I get Bob Hanley away from Joanne Richards?

"Class," Mrs. P.P. said, "history books out, clean paper and pen on desk. We're going to outline chapter two together."

It was Wednesday after lunch. Josh leaned over. "Got a pen?" he asked. "Left mine at the library last night."

Right, I thought as I whispered back, "What happened to the one I gave you this morning?"

"Cioffi took it," he said.

I looked up the aisle to see Cioffi borrowing a pen from Rita.

"I don't have another one," I lied.

"Miss Granger," Mrs. P.P. said. "Will you kindly leave Mr. Greene alone so he can do his work."

I wanted to say, "Then you lend him a pen." Instead I said, "Sorry, Mrs. Peterson."

Just then she was distracted by a knock on our door. While she went to the door, I handed Josh a pen and scowled at him. "It's the last one. Forever," I whispered.

"Thank you," he said with a smile. He gently turned the

pen around in his hand like it was this precious thing. "The last one," he said. "I better be careful with it."

Mrs. P.P. stepped back in the room. All eyes turned to the door because just behind her was this man in beat-up dungarees and an old shirt. He was carrying a little suitcase. I don't know about anyone else, but the reason I was staring at him was because he looked like an older version of Josh Greene.

I turned to Josh. He wasn't paying much attention, like maybe he wasn't seeing the resemblance between him and that man the way I was.

"Josh," Mrs. P.P. said in this very gentle voice. It was the first time she'd ever called any of us by our first names. "Josh, come here, dear. There's someone here to see you." Now Josh was paying attention. He looked at the man, jumped up and ran down the aisle.

It *is* his father, I said to myself. Josh's father had disappeared when Josh was a little baby. Now he was back. Tears were coming to my eyes. Josh wouldn't be an orphan anymore!

Only Josh didn't run to his father and give him a hug or anything like that. He pushed Mrs. P.P. out of the way and ran down the hall.

We were all stunned. I guess by then some of the other kids had seen the resemblance too. The man just stood there staring after Josh. He didn't chase him or call to him or anything.

Mrs. P.P. straightened herself up and in her most even and teacherly voice told us to get back to our history outlines. That she was depending on us to show her what mature young men and women we were. She closed the door, but I could see her head bobbing up and down as she and the man talked. Then she poked her head back in the room. "An old pupil has come for a visit," she explained. "I'll be back in a few minutes. Louise, you're in charge." Mrs. Peterson left our door open and went down the hall with the man I knew had to be Josh Greene's lost father.

But where was Josh?

He didn't come back the rest of the school day. Maybe, I thought, he met his father outside the school and right now they're having a good talk and his father is saying he won't have to live in an orphanage anymore. That they'll get an apartment together. I wondered if Mr. Greene knew that his mother, Josh's grandmother, had died last year or was Josh telling him right that very instant. Maybe he and his dad will bring flowers to her grave.

But at eight o'clock when I came in from walking Willie the phone was ringing and I learned that not one of my daydreams about Josh and his dad was true. The only true thing was that the man at school was Josh's father.

Father Tierney was on the phone asking me if I had seen Josh.

I told him what happened at school, but he already knew all about it. Josh's father was at the orphanage waiting for Josh to come back.

"We thought you might know where he'd go," Father Tierney explained. This was a whole new idea to me. Josh didn't just run out of school. He'd run away!

"I don't know," I admitted.

"Well, George O'Connell thought you might have some ideas," Father said. When I heard he'd gotten George from work and that George was at the orphanage, I knew it was serious, that they were afraid Josh might be upset enough to run away and never come back.

George got on the phone to talk to me and we decided to go look for Josh together. While I was waiting for him to pick me up I made a list of the places Josh might have gone.

62

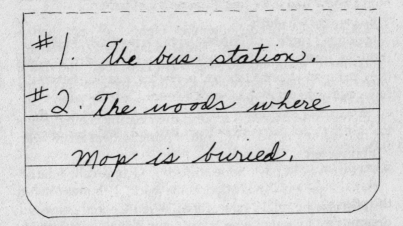

#1. The bus station.

#2. The woods where

Mop is buried.

"Why'd he run away?" I asked George as we headed to the bus station. "I thought he'd be happy that his dad came back."

"He's probably glad," George explained. "But also pretty mad because his father left him and stayed away for so many years. I think Josh ran away because he's confused and doesn't know what to think."

This is what we learned at the bus station: Josh had been there and left when he found out that a ticket to New York City costs fifty dollars.

Then we took the flashlight from the trunk of the car and went through the woods to the clearing where Mop was buried. We couldn't tell if anyone had been there. I mean it wasn't like there was snow on the ground so you could see tracks or anything. George found lots of broken twigs but said they could be from deer and stuff.

We stood over Mop's grave and George flashed the light on the stone that Josh and I had put there the year before. I hadn't been to visit my dog's grave since I'd gotten Willie.

I miss you, Mop, I said silently. Please get Josh to come

back. And let his father be a nice man and everything be all right.

I remembered the September night two years before when Mop and I ran away. The woods were scary at night, and lonely. I sure hoped Josh wasn't out there and that if he was he'd find his way back and not have to spend the night in the woods alone.

George and I walked around the clearing calling Josh's name as loud as we could and waiting to hear an answer. Then we left.

We drove to a pay phone and while George called the orphanage to see if Josh had come back, I thought about where else he might have gone. When George got in the car and told me that Josh hadn't come back I told him my new idea. "Angelo's," I said. "Maybe he went there to sleep."

"We called Angelo first thing," George explained. "Josh didn't show up for work. And if he came later, Angelo would have let Father Tierney know."

"But," I said, "maybe he's there and Angelo doesn't know it. Maybe he went *after* Angelo closed up. Maybe he has a key or knows how to sneak in and is hiding in the back."

George turned on the car motor. "It's worth a try," he said.

As we got closer to Angelo's I got this other idea. "I don't think we should ring the doorbell or get Angelo or anything," I said. "If Josh hears us he might just run away again." George agreed so we parked the car a few doors away and walked around the back of the house. We stared in all the windows but it was too dark to see anything.

"This isn't going to work," I told George. "We've got to get inside."

"You wait here," George said. "I'll go around and ring

the bell for Angelo to let me in. It's the only way. Then if Josh comes out back, we're covered."

"Good," I said.

He started to creep around the house to the front and then turned back. "You better go around the front," he said. "In case Josh makes a run for it."

So we changed places. I knew that if Josh started running George could catch him and hold him, and I couldn't.

I rang Angelo's bell and listened as he came down the stairs to answer the door. At first he was surprised to see me, then he said, "Any word about Josh?" I motioned with my finger to my lips to whisper. If Josh was hiding in the offices I didn't want him to hear us.

"That's why I'm here," I explained in a whisper. "I want to see if Josh is hiding down here. My . . . my stepfather is out back in case Josh runs out that way."

Angelo and I started a systematic search. First the receptionist's area and closet. No Josh.

Then down the long hall. No Josh.

My heart was pounding like I was Nancy Drew or something. All the time we were as quiet as could be. Next we went to the operating room. No Josh.

As we were approaching the room where all the animals stay we heard barking and shouting. It was George's voice. "Josh," he shouted, "Josh, wait. Please." And the sound of rushing and running and Josh shouting, "Leave me alone. Leave me alone."

By then we were out on the back porch, and Angelo flipped on the lights and we saw George catch Josh halfway across the yard. We ran down the steps and toward them.

"Leave me alone," Josh kept yelling.

"I won't," George shouted back. "I won't let you leave us."

Josh was struggling with all his might, but George had

65

him around the chest from behind. Angelo yelled, "You *can't* run away. I need you."

Josh stopped struggling and sort of went limp.

If I wasn't here, I thought, maybe he'd cry and George would give him a hug. But the minute Josh saw me he started to act sort of tough and like it all hadn't happened.

"I haven't wrestled like that since I was a kid," George said. "You're pretty strong there."

Josh sort of shook himself and wiped his eyes with the back of his sleeve. "I could've licked you," he said. "But I was holding back. I didn't want to hurt you."

"Well, thanks," George said as if he really believed it.

I looked at the two of them standing there in the yellow light from Angelo's porch. Josh was as big as George, just skinnier. But I bet he's as strong, I thought. I bet he could have beat George and run away.

Just then Angelo's wife came running out to us. She took one look at Josh and started crying and hugging him. "Oh my, there you were all the time. I was so worried about you, Josh Greene. I'm so happy you're all right."

"They're a lot of people who will be glad to hear you're okay," George added.

"Including," Angelo said, "your father. He's waiting for you at St. Joe's."

I thought that was a bad idea of Angelo's—to mention Josh's father right then. George did, too, because he said, "I think what I need right now is a good supper. How about it, Josh? Want to come to Stangoni's with me?"

"Okay," Josh said in this quiet voice, like he was glad George was sort of taking over.

"Great," George said. "Now, Angelo, maybe you could make some phone calls and let everyone know things are under control here. Tell Father Tierney I'll call him in an hour or so."

"Sure," Angelo agreed.

George reached into his pocket for paper and pen. As he wrote a telephone number he said, "This is my wife's number. I'd be grateful if you'd call her too."

"And my dad," I added.

"Your dad?" George said.

"Yes," I explained. "To tell him I'm with you."

Josh looked at George with this surprised look, like maybe he didn't want me to go to eat with them. And George looked at me as if to say, It's better for Josh if I'm alone with him. So I said, "Maybe I better go home. I have to walk Willie and I'm way behind in my homework from being sick last week."

"Well, if you don't want to come," Josh said, as if he wanted me to come when I knew he didn't.

We were all quiet in the car. I guess Josh and George were waiting until they were alone to talk about Josh's father and what Josh was going to do. I wished I could be a fly on the wall at Stangoni's and hear everything they'd say.

The next morning Josh Greene was at his place in school and everyone acted like nothing had happened the day before. I didn't tell anyone, not even Sue, about finding Josh.

During math Josh handed me a note:

HOW DID YOU KNOW
WHERE I WAS?

I wrote back:

> *I used my head.*
> *I went to the*
> *bus stop too.*

He handed me another note.

> WHERE ELSE DID
> U LOOK ?

I wrote back:

> *Mop's grave.*

Josh nodded yes, meaning he'd been there. He kept the note and didn't write anything else.

I wanted to write him another note asking about his father and about what he was going to do, but decided if there was something Josh wanted me to know, he'd find a way to tell me.

At lunch no one even bothered asking me anything about Josh. They'd already forgotten the man at the door and that Josh had run out. What everyone was talking about was what to wear to the high school Halloween dance. I kept another secret that day. I'd decided not to tell anyone, not even Sue, that Miriam was going to make me over.

I was home from school only a few minutes when my mother called.

"Hi, Mom," I said as I let Willie out of his crate and put him on my lap. He was giving me wet little kisses all the time I was talking to my mom. "What's up?" I asked her.

"Just checking in," she said. "I wondered how you were after all the excitement with Josh last night."

"Okay," I said. "Only Josh and George didn't want me to go to Stangoni's with them."

"Well," she said, "that's understandable. Josh was pretty upset. Sometimes when you're upset it's easier to express yourself to one person. George is helping Josh. He really cares about him."

"I know," I said, and I remembered how when I was blaming Josh for Mop's death George chased him through the park and put his arm around his shoulder.

"Mom," I asked, "what about Josh's father?"

"That's another reason I called," she said. "It's been decided that the best way for Josh and his father to have their first meeting after so long is to have it in a relaxed atmosphere. So George suggested Josh and Mr. Greene have dinner with us tonight. It might be nice if you were here, too. I could use some help.''

"Sure,'' I said. "I'll come.'' This is so exciting, I thought. Our lives are turning out like an episode of "The Waltons'' or "Little House on the Prairie.''

"Can I bring Willie?'' I asked her.

"Okay,'' she said. "But remember you're coming to help.''

"I know,'' I said. "We'll leave right now.''

I quickly wrote a note to Dad and Miriam, put on my red sweater, snapped on Willie's leash, and walked to Mom's.

While we were walking I started thinking again about how nice it would be if Josh's father settled down in Burlington and Josh could move out of the orphanage. Maybe George could help Mr. Greene get a job at IBM or something, I thought, as we started up the walk toward the kitchen door.

Our house looked pretty messy to me after being at Miriam's. I didn't know how Mom and I were going to pick up the house and get a spaghetti dinner made in one and a half hours. Especially since Jelo was colicky.

"No one really knows why it happens to some babies and not to others,'' Mom explained as she walked in circles in the living room trying to get Jelo to stop crying. "Some babies just have a harder time than others.'' She sighed. "And so do some mothers.''

In the end I did just about all the work for the dinner. I made the table look extra special by using a tablecloth and the good dishes. I even found some candles and put them on the table like we do at Miriam's.

"Are we having wine?'' I yelled to my mom. "Because it's special company and everything?'' Maybe Josh's dad would make a toast, I thought. "To my son.''

"No,'' my mom yelled back over Jelo's wails. "George said not to offer liquor at all.''

Before I had a chance to ask why, Josh came in the back door. He was shiny-clean and had on a shirt with a collar.

"I'm early," he said.

"That's okay," I said. "You can help."

This was the plan: George would pick up Josh's dad at the rectory where he was staying and bring him to our house.

Josh picked up Willie. "Hi, No-Name," he said. "You're getting huge." Then he asked me, "Why's Jelo crying?" I thought, at least we agree on *one* name, and I told Josh about Jelo's colic. "It's like an upset stomach," I explained.

Josh put Willie down and went into the living room to see Jelo for himself. A minute later my mom came into the kitchen to help me, while Josh was walking around the living room in circles with the crying baby. Here's the amazing thing: In about one minute Jelo stopped crying.

After Josh put Jelo in his bassinet he came into the kitchen to help, too. As Josh and I were cutting up carrots and stuff for the salad and Mom was making her best homemade salad dressing, she said, "You must be pretty nervous, Josh, seeing your dad after all these years."

"I'm not nervous," Josh said. "I'm just glad he came back. He probably has a real good reason, you know, for not coming before. Like maybe he lost his memory or something. That happens to people sometimes."

I looked at my mom. She bit her lip and looked real concerned, but all she said was, "Maybe." And, "I think you should ask him why he's come now." All the time she was talking I got this funny feeling that Mom knew something Josh and I didn't know. I also thought my mother was a lot more nervous than Josh was.

Josh was the first to hear the car pull into the driveway. "He's here!" he exclaimed.

Mom motioned for me to stay with her in the kitchen. "Why don't you get the door," she said to Josh.

71

"All right," he said in a more controlled voice, like he was helping her out or something.

We watched from the kitchen as Josh opened the door and George and Mr. Greene came in together. Mr. Greene looked a lot better than when I'd seen him at school. Cleaner and in a suit. It was a baggy suit, but it looked nice with a white shirt and everything. His hair was the same sandy color as Josh's, only with a little gray in it. And he had the same sharp nose and high cheekbones. The posture was the same, too, cocky and a little slumped at the same time.

"So hello there, Josh," he said in this deep gravelly voice.

Instead of saying hello back, or hugging his father or any of the things I'd imagined, Josh said, "Where've you been?"

"Places," his father said. "Just traveling."

For twelve years? I thought.

"Well, come on," George said as he led Mr. Greene into the living room, "and let me introduce the family." And he did. He even introduced Jelo and Willie. Then George said, "Why don't we sit down and have a soda or something."

I didn't think Mr. Greene had very good manners because he didn't say anything nice about Willie or Jelo, and when George offered him soda he said he'd like something stronger.

This is what dinner was like: awful. Not the food, but what happened.

Josh kept asking his father questions like where'd he been and why'd he leave and what was he going to do now.

And Mr. Greene never said the answers Josh or any of us wanted to hear. He said he'd gone places. He'd left because he wanted to. And he was moving on.

Mom and George and I just felt terrible right along with Josh. We hardly ate any food. The only thing we could do was wish the whole thing was over and that this terrible man would "move on."

The only question Mr. Greene asked his son was, "Did the old lady leave us any dough?"

The look on Josh's face just then was awful. It looked like he wanted to cry like a baby and beat up his father at the same time.

George answered the question before Josh could catch his breath. "Your mother had nothing," he said to Josh's father. "She left nothing, except your wonderful son."

"Is that true?" he asked Josh. "She didn't leave nothin'? No property? No money?"

Josh just looked at his plate and nodded.

"Then," his father said, "I guess I'll be moving on sooner than I thought."

Just then Jelo started to cry. My mom pushed her chair back to get up. Josh put his hand out to stop her. "I'll do it," he said in this little voice. And he left the room without looking at any of us.

As soon as Josh was gone, George said to Mr. Greene, "How could you do that? Don't you have any feelings for your own son and your dead mother?"

"Nope," Josh's father said. "Don't have none for neither of them." And we knew he didn't.

Just then my mother did the best thing. She stood up and pointed to the door. "I want you to leave," she said. "Right now."

And that's what he did. He got up and left. Without saying, Tell my son good-bye for me. Or, Tell Josh I'm sorry.

As soon as the door closed behind him George went into the living room to talk to Josh, and Mom and I did the dishes.

Josh Greene slept on our couch that night.

The next day I went to school, but Josh and George took the day off. Mom told me why. "George and Josh will talk to Father Tierney about what happened,'' she said. ''And make sure Josh gets to say all the things he feels about that terrible man. We don't want him to bottle up his feelings.''

Well, Josh may have told them lots of stuff, but he never, not once in the eighth grade, mentioned that dinner, or his father, to me.

CHAPTER SEVEN

OCTOBER

Mom	Mom	Mom	Mom	Mom	Mom	Mom
19 M	20 T	21 W	22 T	23 F	24 S	25 S

MONDAY AFTER SCHOOL OUR HOUSE WAS FULL OF tears.

First off, you could hear Jelo crying practically from a mile away. Then, as I came through the kitchen door, Willie started to whimper to be taken out of his crate and walked. "Hi, Mom," I yelled over Jelo's and Willie's cries. "I'm home."

I went into the living room to give Mom an I'm-home kiss. She was sitting on the couch, holding her crying baby.

"Hi," she said as she wiped her eyes with her sleeve so I wouldn't see that she was crying, too.

"What's wrong?" I asked her. "What happened?"

"Nothing," she said. "I'm just tired and cranky. Like John here."

Just then Jelo fell asleep in the middle of a cry. I followed her as she put him in his bassinet. "I'm going to sleep for a little while," she said. Then, without looking at me or anything, she went into her room and closed the door.

I stood there for a while and listened. She was still crying—soft, steady crying. I didn't know what to do. Crying isn't something my mom does very much of. Not in front of me anyway.

Willie barked. I got him outside as fast as I could so he wouldn't wake Jelo up.

When I got back inside I tiptoed over to my mom's room. The door was still closed and she was still crying.

Did she and George have a fight? Was Jelo such an awful baby?

Ten minutes later I checked again. Still crying.

That's when I decided I better call George at his office.

"Oh, my poor Jan," he said when I told him what had happened. "She's so tired from the baby and probably has cabin fever to boot."

"What kind of fever?" I asked.

"Cabin fever," he explained. "Cabin fever is how you feel when you're stuck in the house day after day without a chance to go out. What your mom needs," George concluded, "is a change of scene and not to have to worry about John for a few hours." Then he asked me, "If I took her out for dinner, like on a date, could you take care of your brother?"

Instead of saying, He's not my brother, I said, "Sure, if it'll make Mom stop crying."

When George got home an hour later Mom and Jelo were up from their naps. Mom was sitting in the rocker nursing him. She hadn't bothered to comb her hair or put on makeup or anything, and she had on this old maternity top with stains down the front. My mom looked like she could use a Miriam makeover.

George gave her a kiss and told her that he was taking her out for dinner and that as soon as she fed Jelo she should change.

"I'm baby-sitting, Mom," I said real confidently so she wouldn't know that I was a little scared to be alone with such a small cranky baby. "You can wear my red sweater if you want," I offered.

She smiled for the first time since I'd been home. "Thank you," she said, "I'd like to."

I walked Willie so he wouldn't have to go out while they were gone, George took care of Jelo, and Mom took a shower. Half an hour later she came out of her room looking like a new person. She had on my sweater and a pretty blue skirt she hadn't worn since before she was pregnant, and her hair was all curled up around her face. She even had on makeup, like she used to wear when she went to an office every day.

Mom gave me ten thousand instructions on how to take care of Jelo and said I could give him some formula from the bottle if he got hungry. George wrote the phone number of Stangoni's in big red numbers on the pad near the phone. And they finally left.

As soon as they'd driven away, Jelo woke up. I could hear him moving around in his white, wicker bassinet. Was he going to cry? And cry? And cry?

I looked at him lying there, curled up on his stomach with his back in the air. "You're like a little turtle," I said. "But not quite as good. You can't even crawl."

He gave a little cry, not like he had colic but like he didn't like what I said, that it made him sad.

I picked him up and held him up in front of my face. His eyes were open. And this is what he did: He looked right into my eyes. Like a person, not like a turtle at all.

"Sorry," I said. "Don't take it personally. I was just kidding around. Besides, lots of babies look like turtles. You'll outgrow it."

He scrunched up his face again. Was he getting one of those belly cramps? I thought of what it must be like to be so little and helpless and not know how to talk or even know who everybody is. I put a diaper on my shoulder and Jelo on my chest with his head on the diaper. Like my mom showed me. Then I sat on the couch with Jelo and talked to him so he'd relax and not get a stomach cramp.

This is what I said: "I'm Aviva. Your father is not my father, but we have the same mother. Which means we're related. Sort of. You're going to feel a lot better real soon. Your stomach won't bother you and you'll learn to eat lots of terrific stuff like pizza and ice cream and Chinese food."

He stopped making noises like he was getting ready to

cry. I looked over my shoulder to see if he'd gone back to sleep. But his eyes were wide open, like he was listening. So I kept talking. I told him all about what snow was, and that going to school would be a drag, but that summers were fun.

He put his little hand on my neck and held his head up. I quickly put my hand on the back of his head so it wouldn't wobble and fall off. Since it seemed like he wanted to look at me I lifted him off my shoulder and laid him on my legs with his head on my knees. That's when I first looked at his little hand that had touched me on the neck. It was so fresh and delicate. Like a first flower of spring. A crocus or a daffodil or something.

I put his hand on my hand to see how much smaller it was than mine. A lot smaller.

"And," I told Jelo who was looking me straight in the eyes, "your hands are real little now, but they're going to get big and strong like mine. Your dad and our mom are real tall, so you'll get so-oo-o big that you'll be a good basketball player like me. I might even teach you how to play."

Just when I said I'd teach him how to play basketball, he smiled *right at me.*

"Hey, hey," I said to Jelo. "That's the spirit. Now let's have a little music."

Jelo and I went into the kitchen. I put his reclining seat on the table and put him in it so he could keep an eye on me and I could keep an eye on him. Then I put some real hot music on the radio and danced for him. He loved it.

After that I made myself a peanut butter and banana sandwich. While I ate with one hand, I gave Jelo his bottle with the other hand.

By the time we were finished eating I could tell Jelo was tired, so I burped him and rocked him in my mom's rocker until he fell asleep.

When Mom and George came in an hour later the house

was quiet and I was halfway through my homework. My mom looked like the mom I remembered—happy and relaxed. She and George were holding hands. I was glad to see that George was taller than my mom, because that meant I hadn't lied to Jelo when I told him how tall he would be.

"Jelo was good," I told my mom and George. "He really likes WQZT."

Mom smiled at me, which reminded me to tell her: "And he smiled at me. I thought you said he wouldn't smile until he was older."

"He smiled at you?" she exclaimed. She turned to George. "He smiled his first smile," she said. "At Aviva!" Boy was she excited. I didn't think it was such a big deal. But they did.

All week long Mom and George coochie-coochie-cooed over Jelo. He didn't smile. Not at them. But every time I laid him out on my knees and told him things, he smiled at me.

CHAPTER EIGHT

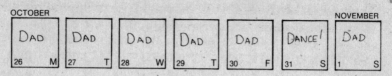

HERE'S THE BEST THING THAT HAPPENED TO ME THE week of the high school Halloween dance: Louise wrote me this note.

> A.G.
>   Guess who broke up with
> B.H.?
>   J.R.!
> He's all yours for the
> Halloween Dance.
>   Your good-news friend,
>   L.K.

Here's the worst thing that happened to me all week: J.G. read the note before he handed it to me. It took Josh about two seconds to figure out who B.H. was and he teased me about it all week. At least *he* didn't blabber to everyone that I had a crush on B.H. L.K. had already taken care of that.

Friday night at dinner Miriam and I planned my make-over schedule. It would all happen at the shopping mall. I wrote down all my appointments.

10:00 Shampoo & haircut at James Hair Salon
12:00 Lunch with Miriam
1:00 Manicure & pedicure at Nu Nails by Lillian
3:00 Makeup from Face First
4:00 Outfit & shoes from Miriam's Magic!

My dad was so bored by all our girl talk that as soon as he finished eating he and Willie went for a walk.

"Why do I have so much time for the manicure and pedicure?" I asked Miriam as we were clearing the table.

"They take forever," she said. "Time to soak your feet and scrape the dead skin from the soles. Then the polish has to be real dry before you put on your shoes."

I didn't like the idea of having the skin scraped off the bottom of my feet. What if it hurt? And if it didn't hurt, wouldn't it tickle? What if I started giggling like crazy all over Nu Nails by Lillian. But I didn't complain or anything to Miriam. I didn't want her to think I wasn't grateful.

The phone rang. Miriam answered it, but it was for me. My mom.

"Aviva," she said, "George is taking care of John tomorrow afternoon so I can take you out for a special lunch, to celebrate your birthday. We'll have a ladies lunch and do some shopping, too. I haven't gotten you anything new in ages. What with the baby and everything."

My heart sank inside me—all the way to my feet. I didn't know what to say. My whole day with Miriam was planned, the appointments, everything. And I *needed* a new look if I was going to get Bob Hanley to pay any attention to me.

"That's great, Mom," I said. "I'd love to, but I have to get ready for the high school dance and everything. Can we do it next Saturday?"

"Why don't I help you get ready?" she said. "It'll give us something specific to shop for."

"But, Mom," I finally admitted as I looked down at my schedule. "Miriam made all these appointments for me. Like at the hairdresser's and everything."

Miriam was loading the dishwasher the whole time I was talking, but I knew she was listening. Just then, as my mother was trying to sound cheerful and saying, "Oh, I see. Well, that's very nice of her," Miriam came over and crossed out her name on the lunch line and wrote in "Mom."

"I have an idea, Mom," I said. "Why don't we have lunch together anyway. Can you meet me at James's Hair Salon in the mall at one? Then you can see my haircut." I gave Miriam the most grateful look in the whole world.

My mother thought it was a great idea and Miriam didn't mind at all because she's so busy in the store on Saturdays.

* * *

"Very sophisticated," Mom said when she met me in the reception area of James's Hair Salon. I put down the magazine I was reading and checked my reflection in the mirror behind the couch.

"Do you really like it?" I asked her. "I mean I've never worn it this short since I was real little."

"I think it's beautiful," she said as she gave me a big birthday hug. "It's just that you look older than thirteen. I don't know if I like *that*. I'm going to miss my little girl."

I look older than thirteen, I thought. All right!

We went to a restaurant on Main Street for lunch. I told Mom I only had an hour because of the manicure and pedicure.

"A pedicure," she said. "How terrific!"

"Isn't it going to hurt?" I asked, "when they scrape the bottom of my feet?"

"Oh, no," she said. "I've only had a pedicure once, but it didn't hurt. The skin is soft from soaking. It's dead skin anyway. All that hard stuff on the bottom of your feet."

"Then it must tickle," I said. "You know how ticklish I am on the bottom of my feet, Mom." Both of my feet were tingling inside my sneakers just thinking about it.

We rushed through our lunch so I wouldn't be late. While I had my manicure with pink-passion nail polish and my pedicure with just a few giggles, Mom went shopping.

I was sitting in the aqua plastic chair with wads of cotton separating the pink-passion painted toes when my mom came in and showed me all the things she'd bought.

4 pairs of lacy nylon underwear for her
4 pairs for me
2 pairs of stockings for her
2 pairs for me
1 flowered flannel nightgown for her

83

1 for me
1 black leather pocketbook. Just for me.

It was the kind of pocketbook I'd always wanted. The right size and with a shoulder strap. "It's perfect," I told my mom as I gave her a kiss.

"Just like you," she said with tears in her eyes.

My mom's pretty sentimental.

Later, as Miriam was helping me pick out my new makeup, I wondered how different I'd look if my mom had been in charge of my makeover.

After pizza for supper I took my bath. Then Miriam came in my room to apply my makeup. She put loads around my eyes. "They're your best features," she explained, "so we're going to emphasize them like crazy." Then she put burgundy gloss high on my cheekbones and the matching lipstick. I prayed I wouldn't be so nervous at the dance that I'd lick it all off.

After that I put on my new outfit. A black skirt with a slit and a gray angora sweater. "I hope there's a special guy to appreciate how great you look," Miriam said as she stood back and watched me get dressed. Even though I hadn't looked in the mirror yet, I knew by the expression on her face that I must look pretty good.

Then I did what I promised myself I wouldn't do. I told Miriam how I had a crush on Bob Hanley, how perfect he was and how Joanne had just this week broken up with him.

"Great timing," Miriam said. "Now take a look at yourself."

I looked in the full-length mirror. It was pretty amazing. I looked at least two years older. "Is that me?" I asked.

Miriam laughed. "It sure is," she said. "You're a great beauty, Aviva. It's time you understood that." Then she told me that when I went into the dance I should be real nonchalant and confident, not self-conscious like I was afraid someone would notice me. I should act like I *knew* everyone was looking at me and that I didn't care.

I practiced when I walked into the living room to show Dad. He got up and bowed like I was a princess in a ball gown instead of a thirteen-year-old in a skirt and sweater.

"Good grief," he said when he'd straightened up and gotten a good look at me. "You look sixteen, not thirteen." That idea didn't please Dad too much. But it sure pleased me.

"You look *so* great," Sue said as we walked down the hall toward the high school gym. "He'll notice you for sure."

"A whole day of people making you beautiful," Louise said. "I'm so jealous. My dad lives in California. I don't even get to meet his girlfriends. Some people have all the luck."

Just before we went through the big doors I checked myself out in the hallway display cases. I looked like I belonged in that high school and I wished with all my heart that I could feel and act the way Miriam showed me. I licked my lips and stood taller as we went through the big doors into the gym.

It was wasted. The only people there were some other kids from St. Agnes and a handful of eighth graders from Cathedral Grammar. And hardly anyone was dancing. Just a few girls sort of dancing by themselves, but you knew they were friends.

"Now that's something we definitely do not do," Louise whispered to our group as we watched the girls dancing. "It won't get us anywhere."

I thought dancing with one another would be a lot better than just standing around trying to think of something to say to people you talk to all the time who can't hear you anyway because the music is so loud.

About ten thousand hours later high school kids started to come. And Bob Hanley was one of them. He came in with a bunch of other freshmen who used to go to St. Agnes and *Josh Greene*. Did Josh tell Bob Hanley I had a crush on him? Would Josh say something stupid about how I had on all this makeup and everything?

"Hi, guys," Louise yelled the minute she saw them. They all waved and the whole group walked toward us.

"So this is the big high school dance," Louise said to everyone as she looked mostly at David. "I don't see much dancing."

"You must have gotten here early," Bob said. "We did that when we were eighth graders, too." He noticed me for the first time. Looked right at me and smiled.

I acted nonchalant and confident. "I guess it takes a while to learn the ropes," I said.

"Right," he said. But Bob wasn't looking at me anymore. He was looking behind me. I glanced over my shoulder and saw Joanne Richards dancing by with a guy who looked like he was a senior or something. Bob's face fell. He looked back at me as Joanne saw him, flashed me this most incredible smile, grabbed my hand and said, "Let's dance."

He led me out onto the shiny wood floor. The song was a fast one that I had practiced a lot with Sue. Bob wasn't as good a dancer as Sue, but he was good enough. I tried to copy some of his moves, but mostly I kept moving to the beat with as many parts of my body as I could get going.

Who could believe it? Here I was dancing with Bob Hanley. I kept saying over and over to that great beat that I knew so well, *He's dancing with me. He's dancing with me. He's dancing with me.*

I saw Sue and Rita standing on the side watching us. Sue

made a small OK sign with her hand. I gave her a big smile and loosened up even more.

When that song slid into another we kept dancing. Every so often Bob Hanley would toss his head and smile at me. *He's dancing with me*, I kept saying to myself. *He's dancing with me again.*

Lots of people were dancing now. Joanne and her older guy were on the floor right near us. He looked pretty bored, like he didn't like Joanne as much as she liked him.

The music softened, slowed down. A slow dance! What will happen now? I wondered. I didn't wonder for long, because just then Bob put his arm around my waist and took my other hand in his and held me close. I was so nervous and excited at the same time that I thought my heart would pound out of my chest. He must really like me, I thought, to dance with me slow and hold me so close.

Over Bob's shoulder I watched as Joanne's dancing partner walked off. He didn't want to dance slow. But she didn't go off the floor with him. She just stood there looking at us. As we danced and turned, Bob saw her there, too. She smiled this inviting smile at him. He pulled away from me, took his hand from around my waist, dropped my other hand. ''Gotta go,'' he said as he walked into her arms and danced away.

I was left standing, without a partner, in the middle of the high school gym as lovey-dovey couples slow-danced around me.

Forget nonchalant and confident. Forget knowing everyone's looking at you and you not caring. I cared. Tears came into my eyes. I was sad and mad at the same time. Sad because Bob Hanley didn't like me after all. And mad, mad, mad that he used me to get Joanne jealous and left me standing alone in the middle of the high school gym with everybody watching.

Because of the tears everything looked blurry. Where

were my friends? What if they were all dancing? I didn't know what direction to go in. A couple bumped into me. "Sorry," I mumbled. As I got out of their way, I stepped on some guy's foot.

"Hey, we're not even dancing yet and you're stepping on my feet," he said. An arm went around my waist, a hand picked up mine. "So," Josh Greene said, "I don't know how to dance, but here I am."

We moved in stiff little circles. One, two. One, two. I put my chin over his shoulder and closed my eyes while I swallowed the tears and regained my nonchalant self-confidence.

I stepped on his foot again. "I don't know, Aviva," Josh said in my ear. "It was between belting that creep Hanley or dancing with you. I figured dancing with you was safer. Now I'm not so sure."

I pulled away and smiled at him. "This is a pretty stupid dance, isn't it?"

"Yeah," he said. "I'm leaving in a minute to go to the movies. I mean I'm not leaving you in the middle of the dance or anything. But when this song is over I'm going to go see *Frankenstein Meets the Wolfman*. It's playing at the horror film festival at the university. Father Tierney gave me these free passes. Want to go?"

We weren't dancing anymore, just standing there deciding what we were going to do while all these couples were dancing around us to this sappy music.

"Why not?" I said.

As we were leaving the dance floor we passed Joanne and Bob. Josh stuck his foot in the middle of their four feet and tripped them all up. We kept walking.

I told everyone I was going to the movies with Josh. I didn't care anymore if Louise and Rita and Janet knew I was Josh Greene's friend. If they didn't know the difference between a boyfriend and a best friend who happens to be a boy that was their problem, not mine.

Then I called my dad and Miriam from the phone in the hallway to say not to pick me up at the high school at eleven because I was going to a movie at the university and could I stay out until eleven-thirty when it was over.

"Are you going with Bob?" Miriam asked excitedly.

Dad was on the other phone. "Bob?" he said nervously. "Who's Bob?"

"No," I said. "It isn't Bob. I don't like him anymore. It's just Josh."

"Oh," Dad said. "I like Josh." Then he said they'd pick us up after the movie and we would all go for ice cream to celebrate my birthday.

As I hung up the phone I looked at my reflection in the display case. Definitely nonchalant and confident. Maybe I'd start wearing makeup to school.

"By the way," Josh said as we raced down the corridor so we wouldn't miss the beginning of the movie, "what happened to your face? You have this green dirt all over your eyes. And your lips look like they're bleeding or something. Is it a Halloween costume and you're pretending you're sixteen?"

"Very funny," I said.

Maybe I wouldn't wear makeup to school after all. Or maybe I'd just wear a little at first, then a little more, so Josh Greene wouldn't notice and drive me crazy for the rest of eighth grade.